ROOTS AFTER SHAHADA

A Gentle Guide for Reverts to Islam — Belonging, Healing, and Growing in Faith

Joyful Hijabi

© Copyright Page

Dedication

To my mother Dorothea— the kindest soul I've ever known.

You lived with quiet strength. You gave with open hands. And you loved with a gentleness that wrapped itself around everyone who crossed your path.

So much of what I've learned about compassion, resilience, and sincere care came from watching you. You helped people without needing attention. You showed up without being asked. You made everyone feel seen.

And even as you were nearing the end of your time in this world, Allah allowed me to be there — to come home at the exact moment He had written. He gave me the honor of witnessing you take your shahada. That moment lives in my heart as a sacred memory — a mercy, a gift, a miracle.

Through the grief, there is peace. Through the loss, there is hope. Because I carry your smile in my heart and your story in my du'a.

May Allah envelop you in light, forgive your shortcomings, and grant you a home in Jannah where every joy is complete and every reunion is everlasting.

And may every reader who finds benefit in these pages become part of the sadaqah jariyah that reaches you.

Ameen.

Table of Contents

Introduction

Keeping My Name, Keeping My Light

To the one who came to Islam, and is now learning how to live it…

This book is for you.

Not the version of you that smiles for others — but the version who cries in sujood, who whispers du'as in confusion, who sometimes feels like an outsider in the very faith that gave them peace.

You already did something courageous when you took your shahada. But no one talks enough about what comes *after.*

About the quiet grief. About the identity shifts. About trying to pray while still learning how to pronounce Al-Fatihah. About missing your old life while being grateful for your new one. About feeling lonely in a crowded masjid. About starting over — with Allah, and with yourself.

Roots After Shahada is the companion I wish I had in my first year as a Muslim. It's not a rulebook. It's not a textbook. It's a heart-to-heart.

When I became Muslim, I thought for a while about changing my name. Many reverts do — and that's beautiful, when it comes from the heart.

But I realized: my name, **Joy**, wasn't something I needed to leave behind.

I kept it because I wanted my life to start conversations, not shut them down.

When someone sees a woman wearing hijab but hears the name Joy, they pause. They wonder. Sometimes they ask: *"How can you be Muslim and still have a name like that?"*

And that gives me the chance to say: *"Because Islam didn't erase me. It illuminated me."*

Your identity doesn't have to vanish. Your story doesn't have to be rewritten. You don't have to wear someone else's culture to belong to Allah.

You are enough — exactly as Allah created you — walking, stumbling, and soaring toward Him.

Each chapter in this book is a gentle guide through the real-life, often emotional journey of what happens after embracing Islam. You'll find reflections, reassurances, some part of my life story and reminders that your path — even with its stumbles — is valid, sacred, and beloved to Allah.

Whether you said your shahada six weeks ago or sixteen years ago… Whether you're thriving or just surviving…

I hope these pages feel like someone holding your hand and whispering: *You're not alone. You never were.*

With love,

Joyful Hijabi

Chapter 1

When the High Fades — Rebuilding Iman After the Shahada Glow

In the early days after you embraced Islam, it may have felt like your entire soul was drenched in light.

There was a sweetness in saying "Allahu Akbar."

A thrill in raising your hands in du'a.

A deep, quiet peace you couldn't fully explain — only that you had found what your heart had been searching for.

And for a while, it felt like that light would never dim.

But slowly — almost without noticing — the emotional high began to fade. The joy didn't disappear completely, but it stopped feeling so overwhelming. Maybe you felt less connected during salah. Perhaps you started to miss prayers. Maybe you began to feel distant from Allah, and you didn't understand why.

And so, the whisper begins: *What happened to me?*

Let's pause right here and take a breath.

You have not failed.

You have not lost your faith.

You are not a "bad Muslim."

What you're feeling is not the end of your journey — it's the natural and necessary beginning of a new stage. This is when your faith begins to grow roots.

The Shahada Glow Is a Mercy

That first stage after shahada — the excitement, the tears, the inner clarity — is a mercy from Allah. It's like the first days of spring after a long winter. You needed that warmth. That sweetness. That undeniable feeling that, *yes, this is the truth.*

But Islam is not a feeling — it is a way of life.

And like any new beginning, the emotions eventually settle. Not because you're broken. But because Allah is inviting you to walk now, not just float.

This is where real growth begins—not through constant euphoria but through intentional effort, habits, struggle, and remembering Allah even when your heart feels quiet.

Even seasoned Muslims go through this — not just reverts.

Even the companions of the Prophet ﷺ once feared their iman had decreased when they weren't around him. One of them, Hanzalah, said, "I feel like a hypocrite." When the Prophet ﷺ asked why, he explained that when he was with him, his heart was full of remembrance, but when he was away — with family or in everyday life — it was harder to maintain.

The Prophet ﷺ reassured him, saying, "By the One in Whose Hand is my soul, if you were to remain in the state that you are in when you are with me, the angels would shake hands with you in your beds and on your roads." (Muslim)

In other words, it is human to fluctuate.

You are not less beloved to Allah because the high wore off. You are being invited into a steadier kind of faith — one that endures.

Iman Is Like the Moon

Our beloved Prophet ﷺ taught us that iman (faith) increases and decreases. It's not linear. It rises and dips, just like the moon. Some nights, it's full and glowing. Other nights it's just a sliver. But it's *always* there — even when you can't see it.

Your iman hasn't disappeared. It's simply shifting form.

Think of it this way: during the early stages of Islam, you were carried by emotion. Now, Allah is letting you *walk* toward Him — sometimes slowly, stumbling — but with sincerity.

And every step counts.

Even when you don't feel the sweetness.

Even when your salah feels mechanical.

Even when your du'a feels dry.

Allah sees every single effort — and He loves it more than you know.

This Is Where Roots Begin

The high after shahada is like a beautiful spark. But if we want lasting light, we need to build a flame—and for that, we need fuel.

This chapter of your life is about learning how to feed your faith.

That might mean:

- Learning a few short surahs to understand what you're reciting
- Praying even when you feel "off" or unmotivated
- Listening to stories of the Prophet ﷺ to rekindle your love
- Finding a regular rhythm for Qur'an, even just one ayah a day
- Attending a halaqah or joining a revert support circle
- Giving yourself compassion when you fall short

You are not failing. You are growing roots.

Roots are slow, invisible, and often messy.

But they're what make trees stand tall through every storm.

You're Not Alone in This

Every revert I know has gone through this shift. Many even walked away from Islam for a season because they didn't know how to navigate the "afterglow."

Some felt like they were no longer "good Muslims."

Some felt unworthy because they weren't crying in salah anymore.

Some doubted if Allah still loved them.

But the truth is that Allah's love isn't limited to how we feel.

He is near when we are joyful.

He is near when we are numb.

He is near when we try — even if we don't know what we're doing.

He says in the Qur'an: *"Indeed, My mercy encompasses all things."*

(Surah Al-A'raf 7:156)

That includes you — right now, even in this quieter stage.

If You're Feeling Lost...

Start small again.

Reconnect with your "why." What drew you to Islam in the first place? What truth softened your heart?

Return to the basics:

- One small sincere du'a a day
- One short surah you whisper before sleep
- One moment in the day, you pause and say, "Alhamdulillah."

You don't need to be perfect. You don't need to feel everything all the time. You need to keep showing up — gently, honestly, imperfectly — for the One who always welcomes you.

A Du'a for This Chapter

Ya Allah…

When the excitement fades, help me stay firm.

When I miss the sweetness, remind me that You are still near.

Plant my roots deep in Your love.

Let me walk toward You even when I feel tired.

Help me trust that I am still growing — even in silence.

Let this new chapter of my faith be firm, sincere, and unshakable.

Ameen.

Heart Reflection

Iman doesn't always feel like a flame. Sometimes it flickers. Sometimes it dims.

But even in its quietest state — it's still light.

Your shahada was a spark. But the real journey begins when you keep walking forward… even after the excitement wears off.

Reflect on a moment you felt distant from the deen — but came back. What pulled you back? What reminded you that Allah hadn't left you?

Sometimes, the softest steps are the most sacred ones.

❀ Heart Journal #1

What part of your faith journey felt the most 'alive' after shahada? What part feels quieter now?

____

____

____

____

____

Chapter 2

Understanding Tawheed Through the Heart, Not Just the Mind

When you first accepted Islam, you may have heard that *Tawheed* — the belief in the Oneness of Allah — is the foundation of everything.

And it's true.

But for many reverts, Tawheed is first encountered as a concept:

One God. No partners. No idols. No intermediaries.

It's powerful. It's pure. It makes sense.

But sometimes, it can feel like something you're supposed to *know* — rather than something you're meant to *feel*.

This chapter is about softening that idea—about moving from the intellectual to the intimate, from understanding Tawheed with your head… to holding it with your heart.

Because Tawheed isn't just a doctrine.

It's not just a point of theology.

It's the heartbeat of your relationship with Allah.

Not Just One God — The *Only* One You Turn To

Before Islam, many of us turned to other things to feel safe. A loved one. A ritual. A symbol we didn't fully understand.

We might not have called it "worship." But it was.

We depended on people more than we depended on Allah.

We believed success came from effort alone.

We thought healing came from time, therapy, or ourselves— but not from the One who created our hearts in the first place.

In its most beautiful form, Tawheed is learning to lean *only* on Allah.

To say, deep in your soul:

"No one can help me the way You can."

"No one can love me the way You do."

"No one can hear me in the middle of the night like You do."

That's not just belief. That's intimacy.

Tawheed in the Life of the Prophet (ﷺ)

When the Prophet Muhammad ﷺ was sent with the message of Islam, the very first truth he taught wasn't how to pray, fast, or dress. It was La ilaha illAllah — *There is no God but Allah.*

But that wasn't just a slogan. It was a lifeline.

In Makkah, when he was being mocked, when his companions were being tortured, when the world around him was turning against him — he returned to this core truth.

There is only Allah.

He is enough.

And He is near.

Understanding Tawheed like this — as a source of peace, not pressure — changes everything.

Your Heart Was Created for This

The human heart longs to attach. To belong. To surrender.

Tawheed gives your heart the only attachment that will never betray you.

Because people will change.

Money will run out.

Health will fade.

Status will shift.

But Allah is constant.

When you understand this, your heart breathes easier. You stop chasing validation. You stop fearing loss. You stop worrying that you're not enough — because you realize that Allah *is* enough and you are already held.

That's the kind of Tawheed that heals.

Letting Go of Spiritual Baggage

For many reverts, Tawheed also brings with it a kind of grief. You may look back at old beliefs or rituals and wonder, *Was that all meaningless? Was I misled?*

But the truth is: Allah saw you, even then.

He guided you step by step. And every sincere prayer, even before you knew His name, was a rope pulling you closer.

Tawheed doesn't erase your past. It reframes it.

You weren't lost. You were being led.

And now that you've found Allah — truly, wholly, without partners — your soul is finally at rest.

Living Tawheed

So, what does it mean to *live* Tawheed in your everyday life?

It means:

- You trust in Allah's plan, even when it doesn't match yours.
- You call on Him first, not last.
- You worship Him sincerely — not out of fear, but out of love.
- You hold your blessings lightly, knowing they come from Him, not from luck or people.
- You measure your worth by His nearness, not the approval of others.

And slowly… you become less anxious.

Less bitter.

Less afraid.

Because Tawheed teaches you that nothing is outside of His control.

Not your past. Not your future. Not your pain. Not your purpose.

A Du'a for This Chapter

Ya Allah…

Let my heart feel Your Oneness, not just know it.

Remove anything I lean on more than I lean on You.

Let my soul rest in the truth that You are enough — always.

Make me firm in my faith, soft in my heart, and close to You in every moment.

Ameen.

Heart Reflection – Chapter 2

Tawheed is more than a concept. It's a comfort.

It's the feeling of safety when you say *"HasbiyAllahu wa ni'mal wakeel."* It's the whisper in your chest that tells you Allah is near — even when no one else is. It's the quiet strength you lean on when everything around you feels uncertain.

Take a moment to reflect: What part of Allah's oneness comforts you the most? Is it that He knows everything? That He controls everything? That He never sleeps, never forgets, never abandons?

Let this chapter lead you into stillness — not to figure out Allah with your logic, but to soften your heart toward Him with trust.

❀ Heart Journal #2

What does believing in One God mean to you on an emotional level?

____

____

____

____

____

Chapter 3

Who is Allah to You? — Personalizing Your Relationship with Ar-Rahman

When you first entered Islam, you learned His name.

Allah.

You said it with awe.

You whispered it in your first prayer.

You held it like a fragile treasure — not yet fully understood, but already beloved.

But in the quiet moments, you may have wondered:

Who is Allah… to me?

Not just who He is in the books or what others say — but in your heart and your life.

This chapter is an invitation to explore that question, to not just *believe* in Allah but to feel a personal relationship with Him— tender, real, and rooted in love.

What Image of God Did You Grow Up With?

For many reverts, the journey to Allah begins with unlearning.

You may have grown up with an image of God that felt distant.

Or wrathful.

Or silent.

Maybe, somebody told you to fear Him, but not how to love Him.

Maybe you were taught that He forgives… but only sometimes.

Maybe you never heard that He listens when you cry at night.

So, when you hear that Allah is Ar-Rahman — the Most Merciful — it might feel new. It's almost too good to be true.

But it is true.

And it's where your healing begins.

Ar-Rahman, Ar-Raheem: Mercy in Every Breath

When Allah introduces Himself in the Qur'an, He doesn't start with power. Or punishment. Or even paradise.

He begins with mercy.

Bismillah ar-Rahman ar-Raheem.

In the name of Allah, the Most Merciful, the Especially Merciful.

These two Names — Ar-Rahman and Ar-Raheem — are so central that they open almost every surah of the Qur'an.

Why?

Because Allah wants you to *know* Him through Mercy first.

Before rules. Before rituals. Before anything else.

He wants you to feel safe in His presence. To feel forgiven, even when you've messed up. To feel loved, even before you "earn" it.

That's who He is.

Speak to Him Like You Know Him

Allah is not a concept. He is your Creator, your Sustainer, your Companion in the dark.

You don't have to wait until your Arabic is perfect.

You don't have to have all the right words.

You have to speak.

Call on Him in your own language. Tell Him what you're feeling. Share your confusion, your fear, your hope.

Say things like:

- *"Ya Allah, I want to know You better."*
- *"I'm afraid. Please hold me close."*
- *"I don't know what I'm doing, but I trust You do."*

This is worship.

The Prophet ﷺ said, *"Du'a is the essence of worship."* (Tirmidhi)

And you can begin at any time. There is no fancy introduction. No perfect setting. Just you and the One who has always been near.

Learning His Names, One at a Time

One of the most beautiful ways to build a personal bond with Allah is by learning His Names.

You don't have to memorize all 99 at once. Just pick one.

Let it speak to your heart.

Is your heart aching?

Learn *Al-Jabbar* — the One who mends what's broken.

Feeling lost?

Learn *Al-Haadi* — the One who guides.

Feeling small?

Learn *Al-Kabeer* — the One who is greater than any problem you face.

Sick or Depressed?

Call on *Al-Shafi*—the One who cures, the One who heals both physically and spiritually.

Each Name is a doorway. A mirror. A comfort.

Write them down. Say them in your du'a. Let them reshape how you see Allah — not as distant, but deeply personal.

You Are Already Known

Sometimes, we don't know how to come close to Allah because we feel like strangers.

But here's the truth: **Allah already knows you.**

He knew you before you were Muslim.

He knew your private tears, your secret prayers, your silent longings.

He knew your past — and chose to bring you here anyway.

You are not starting from scratch. You are continuing a story that He's always been writing for you.

So talk to Him like someone who knows you.

Ask from Him like someone who is loved.

And lean into Him like someone who is home.

A Du'a for This Chapter

Ya Allah…

Let me know You in the quiet moments.

Let Your Names speak healing to my wounds.

Let me love You not just because I should — but because my soul can't help it.

Make my relationship with You deep, tender, and real.

Ameen.

Heart Reflection

It's one thing to believe in Allah. It's another to *know* Him.

To call on Him by name — *Ar-Rahman, Al-Lateef, Al-Wakeel.* To see His fingerprints in the timing of your healing, the silence of your prayers, the unexpected gifts in your life.

Think about the last time you felt protected, guided, or comforted in a way no one else could explain. That was Him.

This chapter invites you to not just worship Allah… But to love Him. To speak to Him. To walk with Him — like He's the closest One to you. Because He is.

❀ Heart Journal #3

Who is Allah to you — not in theory, but in your everyday life?

____

____

____

____

____

Chapter 4

Loving the Prophet  — From Distant History to Daily Presence

When you first accepted Islam, you said:

A*shhadu anna Muhammadur rasulullah. I bear witness that Muhammad is the Messenger of Allah.*

But maybe it didn't feel personal yet.

You believed in him. You respected him. But love? That came slower.

It can feel strange, at first, to love someone you've never met. Someone from a different language, a different land, a different time.

But the truth is — the Prophet ﷺ has already loved you.

And every step you take toward him is a step closer to yourself.

You Were in His Du'a

Let this settle in your heart: the Prophet ﷺ prayed for *you.*

He wept out of love for *you.*

One night, he lifted his hands and made a special du'a for those who would believe in him but never see him. The companions asked, "Are we not your brothers, O Messenger of Allah?"

He replied, *"You are my companions. My brothers are those who have not yet come."* (Ahmad)

That's you.

You, who accepted Islam centuries after him. You, who learned his name long after he passed. You, who are trying, even in this modern world, to follow his path.

He saw you. He included you. He loved you.

More Than a Historical Figure

It's easy to learn facts about the Prophet ﷺ — his biography, his battles, his family.

But he wasn't just a figure of history. He was a mercy walking on earth.

He joked with children. He wept when others were hurting. He stood up when a funeral passed, even if it wasn't Muslim. He forgave people who hurt him — deeply and repeatedly. He ate with the poor and slept on the floor.

And he carried so much weight — not just of his time, but of ours.

Every day, he chose us over comfort. He faced rejection so we could receive guidance. He lived simply so the message would reach hearts like yours.

The more you learn about him, the more you begin to miss him. And that's when the love starts to grow.

Salawat: Sending Peace, Finding Presence

One of the easiest, most beautiful ways to build love for the Prophet ﷺ is through *salawat* — sending peace and blessings upon him.

Every time you say: *Allahumma salli 'ala Muhammad* — you're honoring him. You're drawing your heart closer.

The Prophet ﷺ said, *"Whoever sends one blessing upon me, Allah will send ten blessings upon him."* (Muslim)

Try this: Say salawat in the car. While waiting in line. Before falling asleep. Especially when your heart feels heavy.

It's a simple phrase — but it plants deep roots of love. And with every blessing you send, you're building your connection to him.

Learning About His Life With the Heart

Start with one story.

One moment from his seerah (biography). One hadith that makes you feel seen. One description that touches your heart.

Read about the "Shama'il" compiled by Imam Tirmidhi. It's a way to learn about the Prophet's life and character, fostering a deeper appreciation for his message and role.

Maybe it's the way he said, *"Smile is a charity."* Or how he prayed with his granddaughter riding on his back. Or how he never mocked anyone. Or how he always forgave — even when deeply wronged.

These aren't just traits to admire. They're glimpses of the one whose character was described by Allah as *"an exalted standard"* (Surah Al-Qalam 68:4).

Every trait you learn, every habit you emulate, brings you closer.

Loving Him Without Guilt

Sometimes reverts feel guilty: *"I should love him more."* Or: *"Everyone else seems to feel it… but I don't yet."*

Take a deep breath.

Love isn't a switch. It's a seed. And seeds grow when you water them — gently, consistently, without force.

Keep learning his name. Keep sending peace on him. Keep making space in your heart.

And know this: even if your love for him is still forming, *his* love for you was already complete.

A Du'a for This Chapter

Ya Allah… Let me love Your Messenger with a deep and living love. Let me learn about him not just with my mind, but with my heart. Let me follow his footsteps — not just outwardly, but inwardly. Make his presence felt in my daily life, and allow me to be counted among those he longed to meet. Ameen.

Heart Reflection

What do you currently admire most about the Prophet ﷺ — even if you're still learning about him?

Is there a moment from his life that moved you, surprised you, or made you feel seen?

Write a letter to him — telling him what you're going through, how you're trying to follow him, and what you hope to understand better about his life.

Write a du'a asking Allah to help you love the Prophet ﷺ more deeply and to connect your heart to his example.

Start with: *"Ya Allah, help me know the Prophet* ☐ *not just through books, but through love..."*

❀ Heart Journal #4

How close do you feel to the Prophet ﷺ today? What is your favorite manner of the Prophet ﷺ?

____

____

____

____

____

____

____

____

____

____

____

____

____

____

Chapter 5

Faith Over Perfection — What Fiqh Can Teach Without Fear

When you first embraced Islam, you might have felt overwhelmed by the rules.

Suddenly, there were terms you'd never heard — *fiqh, haram, wajib, madhhab, makruh.*

There were questions everywhere:

- Is this allowed?
- What if I do it wrong?
- What if I mess up my prayer?
- What if I sin and Allah gets angry with me?

And beneath all the questions was often one quiet fear:

Am I even doing this right?

This chapter is here to gently take your hand and whisper: **You don't need to be perfect. You need to keep turning to Allah.**

Because *fiqh* — the understanding of how we practice Islam — isn't meant to scare you.

It's meant to **guide, comfort, and help you grow in love with the One who created you.**

What Is Fiqh, Really?

Fiqh is often translated as "Islamic law." But at its root, it means *deep understanding.*

It's the process of understanding how to live our worship — how to pray, fast, give zakah, purify ourselves, marry, eat, and more — in a way that aligns with the wisdom Allah has revealed.

It's not about memorizing do's and don'ts.

It's about asking: *What does Allah want from me in this moment? And how can I respond in a way that honors Him?*

The Prophet ﷺ once said: *"When Allah intends good for someone, He gives them understanding (fiqh) in the religion."* (Bukhari & Muslim)

So, fiqh isn't a burden. It's a blessing.

Perfection Is Not the Goal — Connection Is

You are not expected to get everything right all at once.

Mistakes are part of the process.

The Prophet ﷺ said:

"By the One in Whose Hand is my soul, if you did not sin, Allah would replace you with a people who would sin and seek forgiveness, and He would forgive them." (Muslim)

That's not an excuse to sin — but a reassurance that Allah *expects* us to struggle, stumble, and return to Him.

Fiqh is not about earning Allah's love.

You already have His love.

Fiqh is about responding to that love through intentional action.

When You're Unsure, Ask with Humility

One of the most powerful tools you have as a Muslim is the courage to ask.

No question is silly.

No question is shameful.

No question means you're failing.

When you seek knowledge, you are honoring your faith.

The Prophet ﷺ said:

"Whoever travels a path in search of knowledge, Allah will make easy for him a path to Paradise." (Muslim)

You don't have to know everything now. You have to be open to learning — slowly, gently, and sincerely.

Start with the basics.

Stick to trustworthy teachers.

Don't overload yourself.

And know that your effort is already beloved by Allah.

Choose Faith Over Fear

It's okay to feel nervous about getting it wrong. But don't let that fear paralyze you.

Take a deep breath and remind yourself:

I am a student.

I am growing.

I am allowed to ask.

I am allowed to learn slowly.

Allah is not harsh. He is not waiting for you to fail. He is watching you try and rewarding you more than you can imagine.

Even a sincere mistake made while seeking to please Him is rewarded.

Let Your Fiqh Be Anchored in Love

Start seeing your acts of worship as a response to love, not pressure.

- You make wudu not just to purify — but to refresh your soul.
- You pray not just out of obligation — but to meet Allah five times daily.
- You give charity not just to fulfill a pillar — but to soften your heart.

Fiqh is not a cage. It's a map.

And Allah is your guide — not your warden.

A Du'a for This Chapter

Ya Allah…

Let me learn this deen with ease and joy.

Let me seek knowledge with humility, not fear.

Protect me from shame when I make mistakes.

And let every act of worship — no matter how small — bring me closer to You.

Ameen.

Heart Reflection

What is one Islamic rule or practice that felt overwhelming at first but now feels more manageable — or even beautiful?

Write about how your understanding has evolved.

What helped you move from fear to faith?

Then write a du'a asking Allah to help you grow in your knowledge and love for His deen.

You can begin with:

"Ya Allah, help me learn with gentleness and patience…"

❀ Heart Journal #5

Which Islamic practice has helped you grow even through struggle?

____

____

____

____

____

____

____

____

____

____

____

____

Chapter 6

Halal and Haram — A Journey, Not a Checklist

One of the most common struggles after becoming Muslim is figuring out *what's allowed and what's not.*

Suddenly, the world is full of labels:

Halal. Haram. Makruh. Permissible. Disliked. Forbidden.

And for many reverts, it can feel like Islam has turned into a never-ending checklist:

- Can I eat this?
- Can I wear that?
- What about music?
- What about birthdays?
- What if I make the wrong choice?

You might feel anxious—or frozen — unsure of where to begin.

But this chapter is here to offer you a different way of looking at halal and haram.

One that is rooted in understanding, compassion, and growth.

It's Not Just About Rules — It's About Trust

It's not random when Allah tells us something is halal (permissible) or haram (forbidden).

It's not to control us.

It's to protect us.

Allah is not trying to restrict your joy.

He is guiding you to a joy that lasts.

Think of a child who wants to touch a hot stove. The parent says no — not because they want to limit the child, but because they know it will cause harm.

Similarly, Allah knows us better than we know ourselves.

He knows the long-term impact of what we allow into our lives.

So when He tells us something is haram, it's not rejection — it's mercy.

The Journey Is Gradual

One of the biggest traps reverts fall into is thinking they must change everything overnight.

But the companions of the Prophet ﷺ didn't transform instantly. The rules came down gradually — over the years. Alcohol wasn't prohibited immediately. Rulings came in stages, with time to process, reflect, and adjust.

Even the Prophet ﷺ said,

"Make things easy for the people, and do not make them difficult." (Bukhari)

So take a breath.

You don't have to be perfect to be sincere.

Let your journey unfold step by step.

Ask questions. Make an effort. Keep turning back to Allah.

It's Okay Not to Know Everything Yet

You are not expected to have all the answers.

There will be gray areas.

There will be disagreements among scholars.

There will be things that feel hard to give up or start doing.

And that's okay.

When you don't know, seek guidance. Stick to scholars and teachers who lead with mercy, not judgment. And never be afraid to ask.

What matters most is that your heart wants to please Allah — and that you're taking steps, even small ones, to align your life with His guidance.

From Checklist to Connection

Instead of seeing halal and haram as a list to memorize, try to view them as conversations between you and your Lord.

Ask:

- *Why did Allah make this haram? What wisdom might be there?*
- *How can avoiding this bring me closer to Him?*
- *What is He teaching me about myself through this boundary?*

This mindset doesn't remove the rules but deepens your love for the One who gives them.

You're not just avoiding something.

You're choosing to trust.

You're saying: *"Ya Allah, I may not fully understand… but I believe You know what's best for me."*

That trust is a beautiful kind of worship.

You Will Slip — And Still Be Loved

There will be times when you fall short.

When you eat something without realizing it.

When you slip back into an old habit.

When you make a choice, you regret it.

But Allah doesn't abandon you for your mistakes.

He welcomes you back every time you turn to Him.

The Prophet ﷺ said,

"Every son of Adam sins and the best of those who sin are those who repent." (Tirmidhi)

You don't need to carry shame forever.

You need to return — again and again.

And every time you do, you are growing.

A Du'a for This Chapter

Ya Allah…

Help me trust that what You have made halal is enough for me.

Give me the strength to let go of what is not suitable for me — even when it's hard.

Make me firm in obedience, gentle in growth, and sincere in every step of this journey.

Ameen.

Heart Reflection

What is one thing you've struggled with understanding or giving up since becoming Muslim?

Write about how it makes you feel — without judgment.

Then write a du'a asking Allah to give you clarity, strength, and softness in your heart.

You might begin with:

"Ya Allah, I want to please You. Help me understand why this matters…"

❀ Heart Journal #6

What is one habit or mindset you are working to change for Allah?

____

____

____

____

____

____

____

____

____

____

____

Chapter 7

Why We Pray — Beyond Motions and into Meaning

In the beginning, prayer might have felt like a mystery. You learned to stand, bow, and prostrate.

You memorized the words in Arabic, maybe syllable by syllable.

You followed YouTube videos and phone apps or stood beside someone whispering cues.

And while that was a beautiful beginning… at some point, the question may have crept in:

Why am I doing this?

Especially when you feel rushed. Or distracted. Or numb.

Especially when the connection you crave doesn't come right away.

This chapter is here to remind you:

Salah is not just an obligation — it's a gift.

A lifeline. A love letter. A moment of reunion with the One who has never left you.

You Were Created to Return

Prayer (*salah*) is not something extra we do when life gets quiet.

It's the *anchor* for the soul in a world that constantly pulls us in every direction.

Allah says in the Qur'an:

"Establish prayer for My remembrance." (Surah Taha 20:14)

Prayer is the invitation to pause — and remember who you are.

Not what the world tells you. Not your mistakes. Not your fears.

But this:

You are a servant of the Most Merciful.

You are seen. You are heard. You are loved.

And you are being called back — five times daily — to that truth.

It's Okay If You Don't Feel It Yet

There's a secret many Muslims don't say out loud:

Not every prayer feels amazing.

Not every sujood brings tears.

Not every recitation stirs the heart.

And that's okay.

Even when you're distracted… even when it feels like routine… even when you're tired and unsure if you "did it right"…

It still counts.

It's still beautiful.

It's still worship.

The Prophet ﷺ said:

"When a servant stands in prayer, his sins are placed upon his shoulders. Every time he bows or prostrates, they fall off him." (Ibn Majah)

You might not *see* it happening, but every prayer is cleaning you, healing you, and protecting you from things seen and unseen.

Salah Is Where You're Meant to Be

In sujood (prostration), your forehead touches the ground — but your soul rises.

Because there is nothing more intimate than putting your head down before the One who raised you.

It's not about performing perfectly.

It's about surrender.

It's about saying:

"Ya Allah, I am Yours. I need You. I'm here."

And He responds.

Even when you don't feel it — He sees it.

Even when you don't cry — He counts it.

Even when you fumble the words — He hears your heart.

Pray Through the Pain

Sometimes, we miss a prayer.

Sometimes we delay it.

Sometimes, we don't even *want* to pray because we feel too far away, too tired, or too ashamed.

That's when you need it the most.

Because salah isn't just something you do *when you're good.*

It's something that helps *bring you back* to goodness.

Pray when you're broken.

Pray when you're lost.

Pray when you're numb.

Because each prayer is a small whisper:

"I'm still trying, Ya Allah."

And Allah honors every try.

Let Salah Become a Safe Place

With time, prayer can become the moment in your day when your soul exhales.

A moment that's just you and your Lord. No noise. No pressure. No judgment.

So take your time. Breathe. Don't rush the motions. Don't rush the words.

Let salah become your sanctuary — the place to meet the One who loves you most.

A Du'a for This Chapter

Ya Allah…

Make my prayer a source of peace, not pressure.

Let me feel close to You, even when my mind is tired and my heart is numb.

Let my sujood soften what the world has hardened.

Let my salah become my safe place.

Ameen.

Heart Reflection

Think of a time when you felt peace in prayer — even a small moment.

What made it special? What were you feeling?

If you haven't felt it yet, what do you hope salah can become for you?

Write a small, sincere du'a from your heart.

Begin with:

"Ya Allah, help me love salah…"

 ## Heart Journal #7

What does a meaningful prayer feel like to you — or what do you hope it will feel like?

____

____

____

____

____

____

____

____

____

____

____

Chapter 8

You Belong Here — Reverts, Culture, and Identity Crises

Sometimes the hardest part of becoming Muslim isn't the beliefs — it's finding your place.

You may love Allah deeply, believe in the Prophet  fully, and try your best to follow the deen…

…but still feel like an outsider.

You walk into a masjid and feel like you're in someone else's living room.

You join a gathering and realize everyone speaks a language you don't understand.

You scroll Islamic content online and wonder if there's space for someone like *you*.

You begin to ask silently:

Do I belong here? Or am I just visiting someone else's religion?

Let this chapter wrap around your heart like a warm hug:

You do belong. And you always have.

Islam Is Not a Culture — It's a Calling

Islam didn't come for one group of people, one region, or one ethnicity.

It went for *every soul who longs for Allah.*

The Qur'an says:

"O mankind, indeed, We have created you from male and female and made you peoples and tribes that you may know one another."

(Surah Al-Hujurat 49:13)

Islam acknowledges culture — but it doesn't *belong* to any culture.

You can be Muslim and Black.

You can be Muslim and Latino.

You can be Muslim and White, Asian, Native, mixed, adopted — anything.

You don't have to "become" Arab, Desi, or anything else to be part of this ummah.

You have to be sincere.

Why You Might Feel Like You Don't Fit

The early days of Islam were filled with converts.

Some were wealthy. Some were enslaved. Some were from the nobility. Some were from distant tribes.

And many of them felt like outsiders at first.

So, if you've ever felt:

- Too new
- Too different

- Too unsure of how to "act Muslim"
- Or even too "American" or "Western" …

You're not alone.

Your feeling is real — and it's valid.

But it's not the truth of your value.

Your worth in this deen is based on your **taqwa** — your connection to Allah — not your ethnicity, background, or fluency.

The Ummah Needs You

Yes — you.

Your voice. Your story. Your presence.

Because every revert brings something precious to the ummah:

- A fresh perspective
- A revived appreciation for Islam
- A more profound empathy for outsiders
- A reminder that guidance is still reaching hearts

You are not just a guest in this faith.

You are a part of its future.

The Prophet ﷺ said:

"The believers are like a structure, each one strengthening the other." (Bukhari)

You're one of those bricks.

This house of faith is stronger with you in it.

Give Yourself Time to Belong

Belonging doesn't happen overnight.

You may grieve your old world while trying to build a new one.

You may try to join a community and still feel like a stranger.

You may struggle with cultural clashes, isolation, or loneliness.

But that doesn't mean you're in the wrong place.

It means you're *building something real.*

And that takes time, trust, and a whole lot of du'a.

In the meantime:

- Make space for the beauty in your background.
- Keep reaching out — even when it's awkward.
- Create a community if you don't find it.
- Remember: Allah sees your effort, even if others don't.

A Du'a for This Chapter

Ya Allah…

Help me feel at home in this ummah.

Remove the loneliness that lingers after shahada.

Let me be sincerely welcomed — and help me welcome others in return.

Make me feel seen, valued, and connected in Your religion.

Ameen.

Heart Reflection

Have you ever felt like an outsider in your Muslim journey?

Write honestly about those moments — without judgment.

Then ask yourself:

What makes me feel like I *do* belong in Islam?

Maybe it's a verse. A prayer. A moment of peace in sujood.

Let that be your anchor.

❀ Heart Journal #8

Write a short du'a asking Allah to help you find your place in this faith — emotionally, spiritually, and socially.

Have you ever felt like an outsider in the ummah? What helped you stay rooted?

____

____

____

____

____

____

____

____

____

____

____

____

____

____

Chapter 9

Learning to Wear Islam — Hijab, Identity, and Confidence

For many sisters who embrace Islam, hijab is one of the most visible — and emotional — parts of the journey.

It's not just a piece of fabric.

It's a public declaration.

It's a spiritual decision that the whole world can see.

For reverts, it can feel like carrying their faith on their shoulders—sometimes before their hearts feel ready.

This chapter isn't here to pressure you.

It's here to hold space for the journey.

Because *wearing Islam* — in all its forms — is deeply personal, deeply spiritual, and sometimes… deeply challenging.

Hijab Is More Than a Symbol — It's an Act of Surrender

Hijab isn't just about modesty in appearance — it's about submitting to Allah in love.

It's not about being invisible. It's about being intentional.

It says:

- "My body is not up for public consumption."

- "My worth is not defined by how I look."
- "I wear this not because society asked me to… but because my Lord did."

That's powerful. And freeing, and also — sometimes scary.

In many parts of the world, the hijab makes you stand out.

It invites questions. Stares. Judgments. Even fear.

So, let's say it clearly: **If you've ever struggled with hijab, you are not weak. You are human.**

And Allah sees the weight it carries.

The First Time Is the Hardest

You might remember the day you wore hijab in public for the first time.

The hesitation.

The butterflies.

The thoughts racing through your mind.

What will people say? Will my family stare? Will I lose my job? Will strangers treat me differently?

And yet — you stepped out anyway.

Or maybe you haven't yet. Maybe you're still building the courage. Maybe you wear it on and off. Maybe you're unsure if you ever will.

Wherever you are in that journey, know this:

Hijab is a decision between you and Allah — and He knows the battle you're fighting inside.

You Are Not a Hypocrite for Struggling

It's common for reverts to feel guilt when they delay hijab or take it off after trying.

You might think:

- "I'm not strong enough."
- "I'm a hypocrite."
- "I don't deserve to call myself Muslim."

But those whispers are from shaytan.

The Prophet ﷺ said:

"Every son of Adam sins, and the best of those who sin are those who repent." (Tirmidhi)

Struggling does not erase your sincerity.

The struggle *is* part of your sincerity.

Keep making du'a. Keep turning to Allah.

Don't give up on yourself even when you're unsure, scared, or inconsistent.

Let Your Confidence Come From Your Lord

The hijab is countercultural in many societies.

It can feel like you're giving up your identity.

But in truth — you're discovering your *real* identity.

Trends do not define you.

Beauty standards do not define you.

Strangers' opinions do not define you.

You are a servant of Allah. A believer. A woman of dignity and strength.

And that's a beauty that radiates far beyond what anyone else can see.

A Du'a for This Chapter

Ya Allah…

Give me confidence in Your commands.

Let me wear my faith with love, not fear.

If I am struggling, be gentle with me.

If I feel judged, protect my heart.

Let every scarf, every effort, and every intention be accepted by You.

Ameen.

Heart Reflection

What does hijab mean to you right now — spiritually, emotionally, or socially?

Whether you wear it, plan to, or are still unsure, write about your honest feelings.

Then write a du'a asking Allah to help you honor Him in your appearance and heart.

You can begin with:

"Ya Allah, I want to please You in how I show up in this world…"

 Heart Journal #9

How does wearing your faith show up in your heart — and on the outside? Do you feel beautiful wearing the hijab inside and out?

____

____

____

____

____

____

____

____

____

____

____

____

____

____

____

____

____

____

____

____

Chapter 10

Your First Test of Faith — Holding On When Life Pushes Back

There's a moment in every believer's life — especially after shahada — when things get hard.

Really hard.

Sometimes it happens right away:

- A family member reacts with anger or silence.
- You lose a job opportunity.
- A friend distances themselves.
- Loneliness or doubt sets in.

And you find yourself asking:

Why is this happening to me now when I'm trying to do the right thing?

Let this chapter remind you:

Tests are not signs of failure. They are signs of growth.

Faith Doesn't Promise Ease — It Promises Meaning

When you said *La ilaha illAllah*, you stepped into a sacred path. But that path isn't always smooth.

Even the Prophet  faced rejection, slander, heartbreak, and pain. And he was the most beloved of Allah.

Allah tells us in the Qur'an:

"Do the people think that they will be left to say, 'We believe' and they will not be tested?"

(Surah Al-Ankabut 29:2)

Your test doesn't mean you're being punished.

It means Allah is strengthening your soul — stretching your heart — inviting you to rely fully on Him.

Every Prophet Was Tested

Look at the legacy of those who came before you:

- Yusuf (as) was betrayed by family and thrown into prison.
- Maryam (as) faced isolation and was accused of things she never did.
- Musa (as) was raised by a tyrant and had to face his fears head-on.

And yet, in every story, we find the same truth:

Their tests became their turning points.

Yours will too.

When It Feels Like Too Much

Sometimes the tests feel heavy — too heavy.

You might feel like walking away from the masjid.

You might stop answering messages from your Muslim friends.

You might even stop praying for a while.

If that happens, know this:

You are still loved.

You are still welcome.

You are still Muslim.

Tests don't make you less faithful. They make you *more real.*

Allah doesn't expect you to pass every test with flying colors. He just wants you to come back to Him, again and again, no matter how messy your return looks.

Let the Test Be a Du'a

Instead of asking, *"Why me?"* — try whispering:

"What do You want me to learn from this, Ya Allah?"

Every hardship carries a lesson. A growth. A purification.

And sometimes, the biggest gift of a test isn't what changes *around* you — it's what changes *within* you.

You become softer. Stronger. Closer to Allah.

That's not a loss. That's a deep, hidden kind of win.

A Du'a for This Chapter

Ya Allah…

If this is a test, help me pass it with patience.

If this is a lesson, help me grow from it with grace.

Don't let this hardship push me away from You.

Let it pull me closer. Let it make me better.

And if I fall — help me rise again, stronger than before.

Ameen.

Heart Reflection

Think of one moment that tested your faith since becoming Muslim.

How did you respond? What helped you hold on — or return?

Write a heartfelt du'a asking Allah for strength in future tests. You might begin with:

"Ya Allah, I trust You even when I don't understand..."

❀ Heart Journal #10

Describe a moment when you faced a test in your deen. What helped you cope?

____

____

____

____

____

____

____

____

____

____

____

____

____

Chapter 11

Your First Doubts in Faith — Finding Answers Without Shame

At some point after shahada, you may have had a thought you were afraid to say out loud.

What if I'm wrong?

Why did Allah allow this?

What if I don't believe everything fully yet?

What if I still have questions?

And suddenly, the excitement of your new faith starts to feel shaky.

But here's something many Muslims are afraid to admit — **doubts happen.**

They don't make you weak.

They don't make you bad.

And they don't cancel your belief.

This chapter is here to give you permission to ask, explore, and seek — without shame.

Doubt Is a Door — Not a Dead End

Doubt doesn't always mean you're losing faith.

Sometimes, it means your faith is **evolving**.

You're not satisfied with surface answers.

You want to understand.

You want to feel certainty.

You want your heart to settle.

That's a good thing.

The Prophet Ibrahim (as) once asked Allah to show him how He brings the dead back to life. Not because he didn't believe — but because he wanted his heart to be content. (Surah Al-Baqarah 2:260)

And Allah didn't scold him.

He responded with a demonstration — because Allah welcomes sincerity, even when it's wrapped in confusion.

You're Not Alone in Your Questions

Many reverts go through a phase where they silently wonder:

- "What if I rushed into Islam?"
- "Why do bad things happen if Allah is so Merciful?"
- "How can I be sure Islam is true and not just another religion?"

These aren't signs of rebellion. They're signs of a searching soul.

The key is to *ask your questions in the right places.*

Seek knowledge from those who are kind, grounded, and trustworthy. Avoid loud voices that mock or confuse. Protect your heart while nurturing your mind.

Islam is not afraid of questions — because truth withstands questioning.

Doubts Often Come With Isolation or Emotional Pain

Sometimes, doubts aren't purely intellectual.

They come when:

- You feel lonely in the ummah.
- You see Muslims acting unjustly.
- You experience hardship and wonder why Allah allowed it.
- You haven't prayed in a while and feel disconnected.

These are not just theological issues — they're emotional ones.

So, before you panic about your doubts, ask yourself:

- Am I spiritually hungry?
- Am I emotionally tired?
- Am I seeking Allah — or just escaping pain?

When you understand the root, you can begin the real healing.

You Can Be a Believer and Still Ask for Clarity

Iman (faith) is not a constant emotional high. It rises and falls.

Some days you feel spiritually alive.

Some days, you just go through the motions.

Some days you cry in sujood.

Some days, you barely get out of bed.

The Prophet ﷺ said:

"Iman wears out in the heart just as clothes wear out. So ask Allah to renew iman in your hearts." (Hakim)

That means even companions needed renewal. So will you.

And every time you return — even with a bruised and questioning heart — Allah welcomes you back.

A Du'a for This Chapter

Ya Allah…

I want to believe with a peaceful heart.

If I have doubts, let them lead me to clarity — not away from You.

Protect me from arrogance, from confusion, from despair.

Let me ask with humility. Let me seek with sincerity.

And let me find You in the end — always.

Ameen.

Heart Reflection

What's one question or doubt you've carried silently?

Write it down — not to judge yourself, but to release it.

Then write a du'a asking Allah to guide you through it with truth, peace, and faith.

You can begin with:

"Ya Allah, You are the Knower of all hearts. Help me understand…"

🌸 Heart Journal #11

What questions about Islam have you carried quietly? How do you cope up with the doubts?

Chapter 12

Your First Mistake as a Muslim — Falling Without Quitting

There's a moment in every Muslim's journey — especially after shahada — when you slip.

You say something you shouldn't.

You miss a prayer.

You go back to an old habit.

You cross a line you told yourself you never would.

And when it happens, the guilt hits hard.

You think:

I messed up. I'm not good enough. Maybe I was never ready for this deen to begin with.

But before you walk away — before shame convinces you that you don't belong — hear this:

Mistakes don't disqualify you. They define your next step.
Even the Strongest Fall

The Prophet  said:

"Every son of Adam sins, and the best of those who sin are those who repent." (Tirmidhi)

Not *some* people. Not *just the weak.*

Every one of us makes mistakes — including you, me, and every pious person you admire.

The difference isn't who sins and who doesn't.

The difference is who returns to Allah… and who lets the shame shut them down.

Your Mistake Is Not Your Identity

One of shaytan's most powerful tools is whispering that your mistake defines you.

That if you listened to music again, wore something revealing, swore in anger, drank, smoked, or acted out — that you've undone everything good you've done.

But Islam doesn't work like that.

Allah is not waiting to throw you out. He's waiting to welcome you back.

The door of repentance is always open — no matter how many times you've messed up.

He is **At-Tawwab** — the One who constantly accepts repentance.

He is **Al-Ghafoor** — the One who forgives repeatedly.

He is **Al-Haleem** — the One who is patient, even when we are not.

Guilt Can Be a Mercy

If you feel guilty, that's not a sign of failure — it's a sign your heart is still alive.

You haven't turned cold. You haven't given up.

Guilt, when guided by faith, is like an alarm clock for the soul.

It wakes you up.

It invites you back.

It reminds you *that you care.*

Let that guilt turn into du'a. Into sujood. Into small steps forward.

That's how healing begins.

Fall — But Fall Toward Allah

The reality is: you will fall again.

But when you do, let your direction matter more than your distance.

Fall *toward* Allah.

Fall into His mercy.

Fall into His forgiveness.

Fall into your next prayer, your next tear, your next step — however slow, however shaky.

Because every time you return, Allah is there.

And He loves your return more than you even understand.

A Du'a for This Chapter

Ya Allah…

I've made mistakes. I've done things I wish I hadn't.

But I still believe in You. I still want to be close to You.

Forgive me. Guide me. Gently lead me back to You.

Don't let my guilt turn into distance.

Let it turn into love. Let it turn into longing. Let it turn into light.

Ameen.

Heart Reflection

Think of one moment you fell — spiritually, emotionally, or morally — since embracing Islam.

What did you learn? How did you feel?

Now write a du'a from your heart, asking Allah to keep you close, even when you slip.

Start with:

"Ya Allah, I fell… but I want to come back to You…"

❀ Heart Journal #12

When you made your first mistake as a Muslim, how did you reconnect with Allah?

____

____

____

____

____

____

____

____

____

Chapter 13

Your New Family in Faith — Building Bonds Beyond Blood

When you become Muslim, you gain a new family. Not by blood, but by belief.

Not always by choice, but by divine connection.

It sounds beautiful — and it *is*.

But it can also be confusing, complicated, and sometimes… disappointing.

Because while the ummah is meant to feel like a home, it doesn't always feel like one right away.

This chapter is for when you're still trying to find your people — and when you're learning how to be part of this new, global family.

The Prophet's () Ummah Was Diverse — and So Is Yours

The early Muslim community was full of people from different walks of life:

- Bilal (ra), an Abyssinian former slave
- Salman (ra), a Persian seeker of truth
- Suhaib (ra), a Roman man who migrated for the sake of Allah

None of them had the same background.

But all of them had the same destination: Allah.

The Prophet ﷺ didn't unite them through culture, language, or nationality.

He united them through faith.

So if you sometimes feel "different" — remember, you're in good company.

You belong here.

Let Go of the Idea of a Perfect Community

You may walk into a masjid and feel ignored.

You may try to join a group and feel out of place.

You may reach out — and get silence in return.

That doesn't mean you don't belong.

It means the ummah is still learning — just like you are.

Some Muslims are kind and welcoming.

Some are awkward and unsure.

Some are struggling with their own wounds and biases.

It's okay to be disappointed. But don't let it **define your faith**.

Because this family, like all families, is imperfect — but still worth showing up for.

You Can Build What You Don't Find

If you can't find your people — be the person you needed.

Invite another sister for tea.

Start a revert-friendly group chat.

Ask a brother if he wants to go to Jumu'ah together.

Be the one who smiles first.

One small act of connection can change someone's whole experience of Islam — including your own.

The Prophet ﷺ said:

"None of you will enter Paradise until you believe, and none of you truly believes until you love one another." (Muslim)

Love starts small. And it starts with *you*.

Your Deen Is Not Dependent on Other People

Yes — we need community.

But your relationship with Allah is still whole, even when people fall short.

You are not alone in sujood.

You are not alone when you recite Qur'an.

You are not alone when you whisper du'a through tears.

Allah sees your isolation.

He sees your effort.

He sees your hope.

And He will send people your way — in time, in His way, in His wisdom.

Until then... you still belong.

A Du'a for This Chapter

Ya Allah...

You gave me a new family in faith — help me feel it.

Surround me with sincere souls.

Let me be loved and loving. Welcomed and welcoming.

And if I feel alone, remind me that You are always near.

Ameen.

Heart Reflection

Who has shown you kindness in your journey as a Muslim?

Write about a time someone made you feel seen or accepted — even for a moment.

Then write a short du'a asking Allah to help you build meaningful bonds in your new family of faith.

Start with:

"Ya Allah, let me find the people who remind me of You…"

❀ Heart Journal #13

Who has become like family in your faith journey?

____

____

____

____

____

____

____

____

____

____

Chapter 14

Your First Year in Islam — Looking Back, Stepping Forward

You did it.

Twelve months ago, you stood still and said the words that changed everything:

Ashhadu an la ilaha illAllah, wa ashhadu anna Muhammadur Rasulullah.

And now — here you are.

Maybe you're still shaky.

Maybe you're stronger than you thought.

Maybe you've made mistakes.

Maybe you've surprised yourself.

This chapter is a moment to pause, reflect, breathe, and realize how far you've come.

Your First Year Was Sacred — Even If It Was Messy

Maybe you didn't memorize as much Qur'an as you planned.

Maybe you struggled with salah.

Maybe you had days — or weeks — where you felt distant from Allah.

Maybe your family still doesn't understand.

But here's what else is true:

You learned.

You fell and got back up.

You said *"Allahu Akbar"* even when your heart was tired.

You whispered du'a into your pillow at night.

You kept walking.

And Allah saw all of it.

Every small act. Every tear. Every quiet intention.

That's not a failure. That's a foundation.

Your Islam Is No Longer "New" — It's Becoming Yours

The first year after shahada can feel like a whirlwind of emotion, pressure, and discovery.

But as time passes, the novelty begins to settle — and that's when something beautiful happens.

You begin to ask:

- What kind of Muslim do I want to be?
- What do I want to keep learning?
- What does faith look like when no one is watching?

This is when Islam becomes not just something you *entered* — but something you *embody.*

You stop performing.

You start planting.

You start growing roots that will hold you for life.

Celebrate Your Growth

We often focus on what we haven't done yet.

But today, take a moment to celebrate:

- The ayah you memorized.
- The prayer you prayed on time.
- The time you gave charity even when it was tight.
- The courage it took to walk into the masjid.

Your progress may be quiet — but it's real.

And it deserves to be honored.

The Prophet ﷺ said:

"The most beloved of deeds to Allah are those that are consistent — even if small." (Bukhari)

You don't need grand gestures.

You need to keep going.

Look Ahead With Hope, Not Pressure

You don't need to have it all figured out by now.

Islam is a lifelong journey — not a one-year course.

There will still be ups and downs.

There will still be questions.

There will still be growth.

But now, you know where to turn.

And you know who you are: a believer. A seeker. A servant of the Most Merciful.

That identity will carry you — through joy, hardship, and everything in between.

A Du'a for This Chapter

Ya Allah…

Thank You for guiding me.

Thank You for holding me through this first year.

Accept every small act. Forgive every mistake.

Let my second year be even softer, deeper, stronger in faith.

And let me always remember: this journey began with You and ends with You.

Ameen.

Heart Reflection

What's one thing you're proud of from your first year as a Muslim?

Write about a lesson, a turning point, or a moment of connection with Allah.

Then write a du'a asking Him to help you grow even more in the year ahead.

Begin with:

"Ya Allah, I want my faith to keep blooming…"

❀ Heart Journal #14

What are you most grateful for in your first year of Islam?

____

____

____

____

Chapter 15

Learning to Read the Qur'an — Slow Steps with a Deep Impact

You've heard it said many times:

The Qur'an is your guide.

It's a light, a mercy, a healing.

It's the word of Allah — revealed to the Prophet □ and preserved for you.

But here's the truth many reverts quietly carry:

Reading the Qur'an in Arabic feels hard.

The script looks unfamiliar.

The pronunciation sounds foreign.

The rules of tajweed seem like a puzzle.

And sometimes… you feel left out of the very book that's meant to include you.

This chapter is here to remind you:

Every stumble, every syllable, every whisper of effort — is worship.

And you are already closer than you think.

The Prophet ﷺ Gave You Hope

The Prophet ﷺ said:

"The one who is proficient in the Qur'an will be with the noble, righteous scribes. And the one who reads it and stumbles through it, finding it difficult, will have a double reward."

(Bukhari and Muslim)

Double reward — not for fluency.

Not for perfection.

But for *trying*.

So if you've ever sat with your mushaf and struggled through just one verse —

if you've practiced a single surah over and over…

if you've traced your finger under the Arabic letters, hoping to one day understand…

You are already earning rewards beyond what you can imagine.

Start Where You Are — Start Small

You don't need to master tajweed overnight.

You don't even need to finish reading the entire Qur'an yet.

Start with:

- A short surah (like Al-Fatihah, Al-Ikhlas, or An-Nas)
- Listening to recitation and following along
- Joining a local or online tajweed class
- Practicing five minutes a day — just five

Consistency beats intensity.

Every letter you learn brings you closer to Allah.

Every repeated ayah is a rope you're gripping tighter.

This is not about speed.

This is about sincerity.

Even the English Qur'an Can Change You

Until you learn more Arabic, don't underestimate the English translations.

Yes — the original Arabic is unmatched.

But even the translation can soothe your heart, awaken your soul, and draw you into du'a.

So read it. Reflect. Let the meanings settle into your everyday life.

You don't need to wait to "feel" the Qur'an.

You're already being held by it.

This Is a Conversation — Not a Performance

Reading the Qur'an isn't just a ritual. It's a conversation.

Every ayah you sound out is a reply to your heart.

Every pause between verses is Allah waiting for your du'a.

Every moment of struggle is noticed by the One who revealed it.

You don't need to impress anyone.

You just need to show up.

Even if you cry out of frustration.

Even if your mouth trembles.

Even if you mess up the same word again and again.

The Qur'an was made for hearts like yours.

A Du'a for This Chapter

Ya Allah…

Make the Qur'an my companion, my light, my healing.

Let me love its words, even when I struggle to pronounce them.

Let it guide me when I'm lost, soften me when I'm hard, lift me when I'm low.

Make every letter I learn a step toward You.

And let the Qur'an live in my heart — forever.

Ameen.

Heart Reflection

What's one verse or surah that touches your heart — even if you don't fully understand it?

Write it down.

Then, write a du'a asking Allah to help you grow in your love and understanding of the Qur'an, one small step at a time.

Begin with:

"Ya Allah, help me walk slowly but deeply through Your words…"

 **Heart Journal #15**

What surah or verse of the Qur'an has stayed with you? What's the first surah that you memorized?

Chapter 16

When You Feel Spiritually Numb —
Reconnecting with Meaning

There may come a time — maybe even now — when you stop feeling much of anything.

You still pray.

You still believe.

But your heart feels heavy… or hollow.

No spark. No peace. Just numbness.

This chapter is here to remind you: **you are not broken.**

You are simply human — and Allah is still near.

Spiritual Numbness Is a Sign to Pause, Not to Panic

Numbness in faith can feel scary — especially after the emotional highs of your early Islam.

You may wonder:

- *Why don't I feel close to Allah anymore?*
- *Why doesn't salah move me the way it used to?*
- *Have I lost my iman?*

But what you're going through is more common than you think.

Even the Prophet ﷺ had moments of spiritual heaviness. There were times when revelation paused, and his heart ached for connection.

This isn't the end of your journey. It's just a new valley in your path — quieter, slower, but still part of the road back to Allah.

Numbness Comes When Your Soul Is Tired

Sometimes, your faith is not the problem — it's your *life*.

You've been overwhelmed.

You've been giving too much and resting too little.

You've been surviving.

And somewhere along the way, your soul went silent.

Don't blame yourself.

Don't shame yourself.

Instead, ask:

What does my soul need right now?

Is it rest?

Qur'an without pressure?

Nature? Stillness? Tears?

Just sitting in quiet without trying to "fix" anything?

Numbness is not always a spiritual crisis.

Sometimes, it's your fitrah whispering: *Come back to the One who made you.*

You Can Still Worship in the Numbness

Faith is not measured by emotion.

You are still worshipping Allah when you:

- Pray even when it feels robotic
- Say dhikr even when your mind wanders
- Recite Qur'an even when it doesn't hit the heart

Allah sees your **effort**, not just your emotion.

The Prophet ﷺ said:

"The most beloved deeds to Allah are those done consistently — even if they are small." (Bukhari)

That includes praying while numb.

Reading one ayah.

Just saying "Alhamdulillah" in the dark.

Even a sigh, if it turns you toward Allah, is noticed by Him.

Let Love Come Back Quietly

You don't need to force yourself into spiritual ecstasy.

Let the love for Allah return gently.

Try:

- Listening to a surah you used to love
- Writing a du'a like a letter to your Lord
- Sitting with someone who reminds you of Allah — even if you don't say much

Sometimes, just being still with your soul is the most sincere form of ibadah.

And slowly, the light returns.

Not all at once.

But moment by moment.

A Du'a for This Chapter

Ya Allah…

I miss feeling close to You.

I still believe in You — even when my heart feels silent.

Please lift this numbness.

Let my faith return with softness.

Let me love You again with joy.

Let my heart beat for You, even if it's only whispering right now.

Ameen.

Heart Reflection

Have you ever felt spiritually disconnected, even while still practicing Islam?

What helped you begin to reconnect — or what are you hoping will help now?

Write a gentle du'a asking Allah to revive your heart with mercy and without pressure.

Begin with:

"Ya Allah, even in this silence, I know You hear me…"

❀ Heart Journal #16

When your heart feels distant, how do you begin to return to Allah?

Chapter 17

Dealing with Islamophobia — Courage Without Bitterness

There may come a moment when someone looks at you differently.

Maybe it's a subtle glance.

Maybe it's a comment under someone's breath.

Maybe it's a bold question that makes your stomach twist.

Or maybe it's worse — a confrontation, a job loss, a threat.

Islamophobia isn't just a headline.

For many reverts, it becomes a daily calculation:

Should I wear this? Speak up? Mention I'm Muslim?

This chapter isn't here to scare you.

It's here to remind you: **you can have courage without carrying bitterness.**

And Allah sees every moment you choose faith — even when it's hard.

They Judged the Prophet ﷺ Too

You are not the first to be misunderstood because of your Islam.

The Prophet ﷺ was called a liar.

A magician.

A madman.

His character was mocked. His followers were attacked.

But he ﷺ never let hatred turn his heart bitter.

He responded with dignity, with truth, and most of all — with du'a.

Islamophobia may feel personal — but it's not about your worth.

It's about fear. Ignorance. Wounds passed down through culture.

You are not responsible for fixing all of that.

You are only responsible for holding onto your light.

It's Okay to Be Scared

Courage doesn't mean you never feel fear.

It means you do what's right *even when you're afraid.*

If your hands shake when you wear hijab in a new place — that's bravery.

If your voice trembles when you correct a stereotype — that's strength.

If you walk into a room unsure of how you'll be received — that's faith in motion.

And every one of those moments is seen by the One who never needs explanations.

Protect Yourself — And Your Peace

You don't have to be a da'wah warrior every day.

You can protect your safety.

You can choose when to engage.

You can step away from toxic spaces.

You can rest when the world feels heavy.

Let your boundaries be an act of worship too.

And when you speak, do it with grace, not to be liked, but to be true to yourself and your Lord.

What You Endure Is Not Wasted

Allah says:

"Indeed, those who have said, 'Our Lord is Allah' and then remained steadfast — the angels will descend upon them, [saying], 'Do not fear and do not grieve but receive good tidings of Paradise, which you were promised.'"

(Surah Fussilat 41:30)

Every rude comment.

Every awkward silence.

Every tear you hold back on a tough day.

It's all recorded. It's all honored.

And it's all part of your reward.

A Du'a for This Chapter

Ya Allah…

Protect me from those who misunderstand me.

Let my faith be a shield, not a weight.

Let me stand with courage, without turning hard.

Let me forgive without forgetting justice.

Let me be firm without losing my softness.

Let my light grow brighter, even when the world tries to dim it.

Ameen.

Heart Reflection

Have you faced a moment where your Islam was treated with suspicion or hostility?

How did it make you feel — and how did you respond?

Write a du'a asking Allah for protection, strength, and healing from any wounds caused by ignorance or hate.

Start with:

"Ya Allah, protect my heart from turning bitter…"

❁ Heart Journal #17

Describe a time when you experienced Islamophobia. What helped you stay strong?

____

____

____

____

____

____

____

Chapter 18

Marriage After Shahada — Faith, Love, and Expectations

Marriage after shahada can feel like both a dream and a puzzle.

You hear that marriage completes half your deen.

You imagine someone who will guide, protect, and love you in the name of Allah.

And sometimes, that's precisely what you find.

But sometimes… marriage brings its own tests, especially for reverts.

This chapter is for the one who is:

- Newly married and learning everything together
- Married to a born Muslim and navigating expectations
- Hoping for marriage but unsure how to begin
- Or healing from a marriage that didn't reflect the mercy of Islam

Wherever you are, this truth remains: **your worth does not depend on marriage.**

But when done right, it can be a powerful path to Allah.

Islamic Marriage Is Built on Mercy — Not Perfection

Allah describes marriage in the Qur'an like this:

"…And He placed between you affection and mercy…"

(Surah Ar-Rum 30:21)

Not control.

Not silence.

Not fear.

Mercy.

That means:

- You're allowed to make mistakes and grow together.
- You're allowed to ask questions, seek compromise, and protect your emotional well-being.
- You're allowed to feel — and be human — within your marriage.

If your marriage feels more like a battlefield than a sanctuary, that's not what Islam intended.

Revert Struggles Are Real in Marriage

If you married someone from a different cultural background, you may feel:

- Pressured to conform to traditions you don't understand
- Shamed for not knowing "basic" Islamic practices
- Confused about your role as a spouse in this deen

It's okay to feel overwhelmed. You're not less of a Muslim spouse because you're still learning.

Marriage is a *partnership* — not a religious exam.

If you need counseling, seek it.

If you need to set boundaries, do it.

If you feel alone in your growth — turn to Allah first, and never be afraid to advocate for your needs.

If You're Not Married Yet — You're Not Behind

Marriage is not a race.

It's not a reward for piety.

It's not the only path to happiness or stability.

You can be complete. Whole. Guided. Loved by Allah — even while single.

If marriage is written for you, it will come in its time.

Until then, work on becoming the kind of soul who attracts sincerity, softness, and spiritual companionship.

And never let community pressure rush you into something your heart and du'as are not at peace with.

My Story: How Heartbreak Brought Me to Allah

There was a time in my life when I thought my marriage was everything I prayed for — but it wasn't.

The divorce was painful. It left me feeling low, uncertain, and unworthy. I questioned everything.

But in that heartbreak, I found something greater: *Allah.*

That test led me to pray tahajjud when no one was watching.

To fast the sunnah days — Mondays and Thursdays — not to earn love, but to heal.

To begin memorizing the Qur'an, not for validation, but for survival.

And in that solitude, I became someone I didn't even know I could be.

Later, Allah gave me a marriage I never imagined — filled with peace and kindness.

A spouse who respects and uplifts me.

Sisters-in-law who feel like friends.

And a mother-in-law who treats me like her own daughter.

But the greatest gift wasn't the new marriage — it was the **sabr** I learned along the way.

The quiet, tearful patience that built my relationship with Allah.

That's the lesson I carry with me always:

Sabr brings more than healing. It brings honor.

A Du'a for This Chapter

Ya Allah…

Whether I'm married or waiting, healing or hoping —

Let me find love that brings me closer to You.

Let my marriage be a mercy, not a test.

Let me feel seen, valued, and safe.

And if I am alone right now, fill my heart with contentment and trust in Your plan.

And if I am married, let it be a union of peace and sabr.

Ameen.

Heart Reflection

Wherever you are in your relationship journey — single, married, divorced, unsure — reflect on what *you* hope for in love that pleases Allah.

Write a heartfelt du'a asking for a marriage that uplifts your faith, not just your status.

Start with:

"Ya Allah, let my love life reflect Your mercy…"

Heart Journal #18

Write a du'a for the kind of spouse or marriage that uplifts your iman.

____

____

____

____

____

____

____

____

____

____

____

____

____

Chapter 19

Balancing Deen and Dunya — When Faith Meets Daily Life

Islam entered your heart like a sunrise.

But then came the schedule.

The alarms.

The work emails.

The dishes.

The laundry.

The kids.

The commute.

The bills.

And now you're wondering:

How do I balance it all? How do I live my Islam when life won't slow down?

This chapter is for that feeling — when you love your faith, but the dunya keeps pulling at your sleeve.

Deen and Dunya Are Not Enemies

One of our biggest myths is that you can't have both.

To be close to Allah, you have to give up your career, hobbies, personality — your whole life.

But Islam never asked you to disappear.

It asked you to be *anchored.*

To work with ihsan.

To parent with sabr.

To study with sincerity.

To live your dunya in a way that *remembers* the akhirah.

You don't have to choose one or the other.

You have to stay mindful of your direction.

Even the Prophet ﷺ Had Responsibilities.

The Prophet ﷺ didn't live on a mountaintop.

He was a husband, a friend, a leader, a community figure.

He repaired his own clothing. He visited the sick. He supported his companions.

He prayed at night — and still showed up for people in the day.

Islam was never meant to pull you away from life.

It was meant to guide you *through* it.

You're Allowed to Slow Down

Sometimes, the best way to hold onto your faith is to pause.

To step back from the noise.

To say no to what drains you.

To protect your salah time.

To delete apps, cancel plans, and create space for your soul to breathe.

Your deen doesn't ask for perfection.

It asks for presence.

And presence needs room.

Make Your Daily Life an Act of Worship

You don't have to be in sujood to be in a state of ibadah.

- Working with honesty is worship.
- Smiling at your spouse is worship.
- Cooking dinner with gratitude is worship.
- Resting with the intention to renew your strength — that's worship too.

The secret isn't changing your whole life.

It's changing the *intention* behind your life.

Say to yourself before each task:

"I'm doing this for Allah."

Yes — even while folding laundry.

Even while replying to messages.

Even while washing dishes.

This simple intention shifts everything.

It brings presence into the moment.

It turns mundane tasks into acts of love.

It fills your day with purpose.

When you dedicate each action to Allah, you stop moving for deadlines and start driving for devotion.

And that's when even the dishes feel lighter — because you're doing them *for Him.*

A Du'a for This Chapter

Ya Allah…

Help me live in this world without being lost in it.

Let my daily tasks carry the scent of worship.

Let my work, my words, and my responsibilities draw me closer to You.

And when I'm overwhelmed, help me return to stillness — with You.

Ameen.

Heart Reflection

What part of your daily life feels the hardest to balance with your deen?

Write about one intention you want to carry with you tomorrow — even during chores, work, or errands.

Then write a du'a starting with:

"Ya Allah, let me live today in a way that remembers the akhirah…"

🌸 Heart Journal #19

How can you bring more worship into your everyday routines?

Chapter 20

When You're the Only Muslim at Work

You walk into the break room and hesitate before saying *Bismillah.*

You wonder if you'll be asked about what you're wearing — again.

You quietly look for a private corner to pray during your lunch break.

You politely decline the office party drinks, or the potluck dishes you can't eat.

You smile, even when the comments sting a little.

And deep down, you wonder:

Am I always going to feel like the only one?

This chapter is for that experience — of being the **only Muslim at work**, trying to honor your deen in a space that doesn't always understand it.

You're Not Just Seen by Colleagues — Allah sees you

Every time you represent Islam in your workplace, even if it's subtle — Allah sees it.

When you keep your wudu for dhuhr prayer between meetings…

When you fast and still show up with energy…

When you choose honesty in your tasks, kindness in your emails, patience when others test you…

These aren't just "work ethics."

They're acts of worship.

And when you feel alone — like no one at work understands the way you live — remember:

Allah understands. He placed you there on purpose.

You're Not Just an Employee — You're a Light

The Prophet ﷺ said:

"Let the one who is present inform the one who is absent." (Bukhari)

In a workplace full of small talk and surface-level connections, your presence as a Muslim is more meaningful than you may realize.

Your peace.

Your manners.

Your refusal to gossip.

Your gentle way of saying *"No, thank you"* to things that don't align with your values.

These are all forms of da'wah.

You don't need to preach.

Just be sincere. Be kind. Be consistent.

People will notice.

People do Not Just see you — Allah sees you

When you're the only Muslim in the room, it can feel isolating.

But remember — you're never actually alone.

Allah says:

"And He is with you wherever you are, and Allah is the All-Seeing of what you do."

(Surah Al-Hadid 57:4)

Even if no one else understands why you excuse yourself to pray…

Even if your family still doesn't "get" your lifestyle changes…

Even if your co-workers or classmates think you're strange…

Allah sees your quiet strength.

And every small sacrifice you make — every awkward moment you bear with grace — is counted by Him.

That's why I chose to keep my name — Joy — instead of adopting a traditional Arabic name.

When people see me in hijab but hear my name, they pause.

They ask. They wonder.

And that opens a conversation — a gentle beginning to da'wah.

I wanted to be approachable, to plant a seed in someone's heart without intimidating them.

To show them that Islam is not a culture — it's a calling.

That you don't have to erase who you are to belong to Allah.

So yes — you might feel like you don't "match" sometimes.

But maybe you're not meant to blend in.

Maybe you're meant to *shine differently — for a reason.*

You weren't placed in that room by accident.

Sometimes, your presence *is* the dawah.

Your calm, kindness, and character — all of it plants seeds, even if you never speak about Islam.

And one day, someone might come to you and say:

"You're the first Muslim I ever really saw. And you made me curious."

That's no small thing.

Your Patience Is Building Paradise

The Qur'an says:

"So be patient. Indeed, the promise of Allah is truth…"

(Surah Ar-Rum 30:60)

Every moment you stay true to your Islam — even when it would be easier to hide it — is a moment recorded by the angels.

You're not just clocking in and out of work.

You're writing a legacy of quiet faithfulness.

And Allah is closer to you than any boss, team, or policy ever could be.

You're allowed to say: *"I need a break from being the only one."*

Find your people, even if it's just one or two.

Make du'a for companionship rooted in faith.

Give yourself time to recharge — spiritually and emotionally.

Your Loneliness Is a Bridge to Allah

When you feel misunderstood…

When no one else around you prays, fasts, or believes…

When you long for someone who *gets it*…

That's when Allah becomes your closest friend.

Turn that loneliness into sujood.

Turn that longing into du'a.

Turn that pain into purpose.

Because your experience — though quiet and hidden — is honored in the heavens.

A Du'a for This Chapter

Ya Allah…

In the rooms where I feel alone, be my company.

In the spaces where I feel strange, be my comfort.

Let my difference be da'wah. Let my silence be sabr.

Let me walk into every room with You by my side.

Ameen.

Heart Reflection

Think of a time you felt like "the only one" in a space — at work, in your family, at school.

What helped you hold on? What made it hard?

Now write a du'a asking Allah for courage, connection, and reward for your quiet sacrifices.

Begin with:

"Ya Allah, help me be strong in places where I feel alone…"

Heart Journal #20

What helps you stay grounded at work when you're the only Muslim?

Chapter 21

When You Fall in Love with the Qur'an

After all the struggle, repetition, and uncertainty, there is a moment when something shifts.

You hear a verse that feels like it was written just for you.

You recite slowly, and the words land deeper than before.

You open the Qur'an — not because you *should*, but because your heart *wants* to.

And then you realize:

You've fallen in love with the Qur'an.

It didn't happen overnight.

You didn't need perfect tajweed or full understanding.

It came quietly. Softly. Authentically.

And now, the Qur'an is not just a book — it's your companion.

It Didn't Start With Love — And That's Okay

In the beginning, it might have felt forced.

You read because you had to.

You struggled through the Arabic.

You relied on translations.

You felt disconnected.

And sometimes, guilt whispered:

"Why don't you feel more? Why isn't this easier?"

But you kept showing up.

You kept listening. You kept repeating. You kept trying.

And Allah responded.

Because *when you approach the Qur'an with sincerity — even just a little — it meets you with mercy.*

The Qur'an Begins to Speak to You

It doesn't speak in your native language, but somehow… it still understands you.

It answers questions you didn't know how to ask.

It soothes wounds you couldn't put into words.

It reflects your life back to you — with wisdom and calm.

You read about the struggles of the Prophets and feel seen.

You read about Allah's mercy and feel safe.

You read an ayah over and over… and suddenly, it clicks.

This is no ordinary book.

This is revelation. This is remembrance. This is a rescue.

And you've tasted its sweetness.

A Personal Reflection

One surah I return to again and again is **Surah Ar-Rahman**. It's hard to explain, but it feels like a conversation with my heart. The repeated question **"Which of the favors of your Lord will you deny?"** softens me every time. It feels like a whisper from

Allah, reminding me of His mercy even when I feel overwhelmed or undeserving.

There have been moments when I was struggling with a question, a doubt, or a sadness… and I would open the Qur'an, just looking for peace. And somehow, the verse I landed on felt like it was meant for me. Not in a superstitious way — but in a way that made me feel seen.

I used to wonder, *"Is this allowed? Is it okay to read the Qur'an like that — like Allah is speaking directly to me?"*

But I've learned that the Qur'an is called **a guidance** for a reason. And when you approach it sincerely, longing for connection, Allah can guide your heart in the gentlest ways.

It doesn't always answer with logic. Sometimes it answers with beauty. With comfort. With presence.

And that's how I began to fall in love with it — not just for its rules or recitations, but for its *presence* in my life.

Let the Qur'an Be a Part of Your Day, Not Just Your Rituals

The more you love it, the more you'll crave it.

Not just in salah, but in:

- Commutes
- Bedtime reflections
- Walks in nature
- Breaks between tasks
- Moments of anxiety or joy

Let the Qur'an be your soundtrack, your comfort, your anchor.

Some days it will feel deep. Some days it won't. But the love doesn't disappear — it just rests, then returns.

You're Not Behind. You're Becoming.

Whether you've memorized one ayah or one juz,

Whether you read Arabic fluently or still trace each letter,

Whether you listen more than you recite —

You are in a relationship with the Book of Allah.

And the Prophet ﷺ said:

"The best of you are those who learn the Qur'an and teach it." (Bukhari)

You're on that path.

And every ayah is a step closer to your Lord.

A Du'a for This Chapter

Ya Allah…

Let me fall deeper in love with Your words.

Let me hear the Qur'an with my soul.

Let it be my reminder, my rest, my roadmap.

Let it guide me in my joy and hold me in my sorrow.

Let me live by it, rise by it, and be among the people of Qur'an.

Ameen.

Heart Reflection

What's one surah, verse, or moment with the Qur'an that moved you unexpectedly?

Write about how it felt.

Then write a du'a asking Allah to let your relationship with His Book grow sweeter, stronger, and more constant with time.

Begin with:

"Ya Allah, let Your words live in my heart..."

❀ Heart Journal #21

Describe the moment when the Qur'an first moved you. Was it a verse? A recitation? A translation? What did it make you feel — and what do you want your relationship with the Qur'an to become?

____

____

____

____

____

____

____

____

____

____

____

____

____

____

____

____

Chapter 22

Trusting Allah When You Lose Friends After Shahada

When you embrace Islam, you may expect resistance from the world — but you rarely expect it from your closest friends.

Yet sometimes, after shahada, the phone gets quiet. The group chats fade. The invitations stop coming.

You wonder if you've done something wrong. You wonder if they ever really knew you at all. You wonder if you're losing pieces of yourself you didn't intend to lose.

This chapter is here to tell you:

It's okay to grieve. It's okay to outgrow. And it's more than okay to trust that Allah is making space for better.

Friendship Loss Hurts Because You Loved Sincerely

You didn't just lose contacts. You lost shared memories. Inside jokes. Late-night talks. Safe spaces.

And sometimes, you're not even rejected with words — you're rejected with silence.

The Prophet ﷺ knew that pain too. When he called his people to Islam, some of his closest tribe members turned against him. Family ties strained. Friendships dissolved.

This isn't a punishment. It's part of walking a new road — one where not everyone can come with you.

Not Everyone Is Meant for Every Chapter of Your Story

Sometimes, losing people is not a betrayal — it's a redirection.

It's Allah gently removing those who could not walk where you are headed.

Maybe their role in your story was only meant for a season. Maybe their presence would have made you shrink, compromise, or doubt. Maybe you needed empty space in your life to make room for the new family Allah is sending you.

It hurts. But it also frees you.

True Companionship Comes Later — and It's Sweeter

When Allah replaces the friends you lost, He sends you souls who love you *for His sake.*

You'll find people who:

- Remind you to pray, not gossip.
- Celebrate your iman, not mock it.
- Sit with you in hardship, not just happiness.

And that bond — rooted in faith — is deeper than any friendship built only on hobbies, humor, or history.

The Prophet ﷺ said: *"A man is upon the religion of his close friend, so let one of you look at whom he befriends."* (Abu Dawood)

Trust that the loneliness now is planting seeds for companionship later.

✦ A Moment from My Journey

There was a sister I was close to — a revert like me. We leaned on each other in those early months of faith, learning how to pray, encouraging each other to keep going when it felt hard. We both made big changes in our lives, believing that Islam would bring healing.

But then… life happened. She went through a difficult divorce. She felt betrayed, broken, and isolated. And eventually, she left Islam.

I still remember how my heart sank when I found out. I wasn't angry. I was just… grieving. Grieving for the friend I had known, for the faith we once shared, for the pain that pushed her away. It made me question things, too. It made me wonder: *Would I make it through if I ever went through something like that?*

In those quiet, heavy moments, I would turn to the Qur'an. Not looking for rulings or fatwas — just comfort. And somehow, the verses I came across would soften my chest just enough to keep me going. They reminded me that pain is part of the journey — but so is healing.

The Qur'an became my anchor when everything else felt uncertain.

And even though my friend walked away, I still make du'a for her. Because I know Allah never truly leaves us — even when we walk away from Him.

Let Your Loneliness Be an Invitation to Allah

In the spaces where friends used to be, let du'a bloom. In the silences where laughter used to be, let Qur'an echo.

Talk to Allah the way you once talked to friends. Cry to Him. Joke with Him. Share your day with Him.

Because the One who listens without judgment is closer to you than your own soul.

And He never turns away.

A Du'a for This Chapter

Ya Allah… Heal the parts of me that ache from losing people I loved. Fill the empty places with Your closeness. Send me companions who will love me for Your sake. And let my heart trust Your replacements — even when I can't yet see them. Ameen.

Heart Reflection

Think of one friendship you lost — or one friendship that quietly faded after you became Muslim.

Write a du'a asking Allah to heal your heart, bless those people with goodness, and send you new friends who love you for who you are now. Also ask Allah to send you friendships rooted in faith.

Begin with: *"Ya Allah, replace what I lost with what is better for my deen and my heart…"*

❀ Heart Journal #22

Think of a friendship you lost — or one that faded — after embracing Islam. How did that loss shape you?

Chapter 23

Building a Home Around Faith — Even if You Live Alone

Islam isn't just something you practice outwardly. It's something you *live with* — inside your very space.

After shahada, one of the most powerful things you can do is create a home that feels like a sanctuary. A place where your soul can breathe. A place where Allah's remembrance feels natural.

But what if you're alone? What if your family isn't Muslim? What if you live in a small apartment, a college dorm, or a room you're renting?

This chapter is here to remind you: **you can build a home around your faith — no matter how big or small your space is.**

Your Home Is Your First Masjid

The Prophet  said: *"The whole earth has been made a masjid (place of prostration) for me."* (Bukhari)

That means even your bedroom floor can be a sacred space.

You don't need a massive library of Islamic books. You don't need Arabic calligraphy on every wall.

You just need intention.

You can begin by:

- Having a clean spot designated for salah
- Keeping a Qur'an nearby, even if it's a translation
- Playing Qur'an recitation softly while you work or rest
- Lighting a candle, opening a window — letting peace settle into your air

Small changes. Big impact.

Your home becomes a place where angels feel welcome. And where you feel safe to reconnect with Allah — however quietly.

You're Allowed to Make It Beautiful

Islam loves beauty.

The Prophet ﷺ said: *"Indeed, Allah is Beautiful and loves beauty."* (Muslim)

So beautify your space in a way that lifts your heart.

Hang a simple ayah that speaks to you. Frame a du'a that brings you peace. Arrange your prayer clothes or prayer mat with care.

It's not about perfection. It's about presence.

When you enter your home and your heart remembers Allah — that's success.

If Your Family Isn't Muslim

If you live with family who don't share your faith, it can feel tricky.

Maybe you don't control the space. Maybe there are things around you that don't align with your values.

That's okay.

Even the Prophet ﷺ lived for years among people who didn't yet believe.

Do what you can:

- Create a small prayer corner
- Keep your Qur'an close to you
- Whisper du'a under your breath as you move around
- Smile with patience, even when you feel out of place

Your faith is not fragile. It's strong enough to glow quietly, even in spaces that aren't built for it — yet.

And maybe, your peace will be the seed that softens other hearts too.

A Du'a for This Chapter

Ya Allah… Make my home a place of peace. Fill its walls with Your light. Let every corner of my space remember You. And if I am living with others who don't share my faith, let my presence be a silent da'wah, and my patience be a reflection of Your mercy. Ameen.

Heart Reflection

What small change could you make today to invite more faith into your living space?

Write a du'a asking Allah to bless your home — whether it's a mansion or a small, rented room — and make it a sanctuary of peace and worship.

Begin with: *"Ya Allah, let my home be a place where hearts remember You…"*

❀ Heart Journal #23

What would your ideal "faith-filled" home feel like — peaceful, vibrant, comforting? Describe what you can start doing now to create that space, even in small ways.

Chapter 24

Loving Family Who Don't Accept Your Islam

They raised you. They fed you. They loved you the best way they knew how.

And yet... when you embraced Islam, something shifted. A distance grew where warmth used to be. A silence where laughter once lived.

Sometimes it's confusion. Sometimes it's disappointment. Sometimes it's outright rejection.

And you're left wondering:

How do I love them — even when they can't seem to love this part of me?

This chapter is here to hold that ache gently.

Their Reaction Is About Their Fear — Not Your Failure

When your family reacts negatively to your Islam, it often isn't hatred.

It's fear.

- Fear that you're leaving them behind.
- Fear that you're rejecting their culture or upbringing.
- Fear of what they don't understand.

Their anger often masks sadness. Their distance often hides confusion.

You are not a bad child. You are not a failure. You have not betrayed your roots.

You have simply answered the call of your soul.

And that's something to be honored — not hidden.

You Can Love Them Without Compromising Your Faith

Loving your family doesn't mean diluting your deen.

You can:

- Visit them with kindness
- Help them with patience
- Celebrate their humanity
- Set gentle boundaries when needed

And you can do all of this while still praying, fasting, dressing modestly, and remembering Allah openly.

The Prophet ﷺ taught us: *"Repay the bad treatment of relatives with good treatment."* (Tirmidhi)

You don't erase yourself to keep the peace. You *become* peace, with Allah's help.

You Don't Have to Force Understanding

You want them to understand. You long for them to see the beauty you found.

But guidance is in Allah's hands, not yours.

The Prophet Nuh (as) preached to his son for years — and yet, his son chose disbelief. Even the most eloquent, loving, prophetic heart could not guarantee guidance for those he loved.

Your role is to show Islam through your character, not to win every argument.

Sometimes, the best da'wah is a *patient, peaceful presence.*

You're Still Their Child — and Allah Sees Your Loyalty

Even if they don't celebrate your shahada, you can still:

- Make du'a for them
- Visit them when you can
- Honor them respectfully
- Love them — even through your tears

Allah honors your loyalty.

And every moment you bite your tongue, every time you choose patience over pride, every silent du'a for their hearts — it's recorded with your Lord.

Nothing is wasted.

✦ A Story That Touched My Heart

I have a dear friend whose daughter embraced Islam while still in university. Her decision took her parents by complete surprise. They didn't see it coming — especially when she later shared that she had met a young Muslim man on campus who would become her husband.

At first, her parents reacted with fear and confusion. They worried she had been pressured. They questioned whether she really knew what she was doing. They even considered it a phase.

But what followed wasn't defiance or debate. It was something softer. Subtler. Stronger.

They watched their daughter change — not just in outward appearance, but in her character. She was more composed. More respectful. She began helping at home without being asked. She listened more, argued less. She prayed quietly, without trying to convince them of anything.

And slowly… that softness did something.

It made them curious. Then reflective. Then open.

Years later, both of her parents took their shahada. Not because their daughter tried to prove anything — but because she lived Islam so beautifully that it invited them in.

Her transformation became their doorway to faith. And to this day, my friend says she never imagined that the light of Islam would enter their home… through their daughter's quiet example.

A Du'a for This Chapter

Ya Allah… You chose my family for me. You placed me in their care long before I knew Your name. Help me love them even when they don't understand. Soften their hearts. Heal their fears. Let my patience and respect be a bridge to Your light. And if I must carry this loneliness, let it draw me closer to You. Ameen.

Heart Reflection

Think of a moment when a family interaction about your Islam felt painful.

Write a du'a asking Allah to heal both your heart and theirs — to build bridges where hurt now stands.

Begin with: *"Ya Allah, guide them, forgive them, and help me love them with wisdom and grace…"*

✿ Heart Journal #24

Write a letter you'll never send to a family member who struggles with your Islam. Say what your heart needs to say, with love, boundaries, and honesty. Then make a du'a for their guidance and your healing.

Chapter 25

Embracing Your Unique Journey Without Comparison

You see someone who reverted just a few months ago — and they've already memorized five surahs.

You hear a sister fluently reciting Arabic, and you wonder if you'll ever sound like that.

You watch someone fasting Monday and Thursday, praying tahajjud, volunteering — and you start to shrink inside.

You start to wonder:

"Am I behind? Am I doing enough? Am I even a good Muslim?"

This chapter is for those quiet comparisons that creep in — even when your intentions are pure.

Comparison Is a Thief in Disguise

It doesn't always show up loudly.

Sometimes it arrives as admiration… that slowly turns into self-doubt.

But Allah never asked you to be someone else.

He asked you to be *you* — on your path, in your timing, with your heart.

He doesn't love you based on someone else's accomplishments.

He loves you for your sincerity.

The Prophet ﷺ said:

"Deeds are judged by intentions…" (Bukhari and Muslim)

You're not in competition.

You're not in competition. You're in a personal, intimate connection — with your Lord, and with your own becoming.

Your Islam Isn't Meant to Look Like Everyone Else's

Some people fall in love with Qur'an first.

Others find strength in hijab.

Some connect through volunteering, or through tears in du'a, or through the discipline of salah.

It's not about being the "best" Muslim in someone else's eyes.

It's about *becoming the believer Allah knows you can be* — day by day.

And that might look slow.

That might look quiet.

That might look different from the people around you.

But it's still sacred.

Celebrate Small Wins That No One Else Sees

Maybe you didn't pray all five — but you didn't give up.

Maybe you finally asked a question you were afraid to voice.

Maybe you went to the masjid after months of hesitation.

Maybe you whispered *Alhamdulillah* through tears after a hard day.

These are victories.

Invisible to others. But precious to Allah.

You're not behind.

You're blooming — even if no one sees the roots yet.

✦ When Competing Becomes Comparison

Sometimes, we hear that *"the best of you is the one who does the most,"* and we take it as a challenge. We see others memorizing Qur'an faster, praying more, learning Arabic fluently — and we start feeling behind.

A little motivation can be good. But if it turns into self-doubt or jealousy, it stops serving us. And it stops being sincere.

Faith isn't a race to the finish line. It's a quiet journey between you and Allah. And what matters most isn't how fast you move — but how honest your steps are.

There were times I compared myself, too. I would wonder, *"Why is her iman so strong and mine feels shaky?"* But I realized something: we're all climbing different mountains, and some people have had a head start.

What brings peace is knowing that **Allah only asks you to try — not to be better than anyone else.**

There's space for everyone to grow. And your pace is still sacred.

Allah Loves You for Your Effort, Not Your Pace

The Qur'an doesn't say: *"Compete with others."*

It says:

"…So, race toward forgiveness from your Lord…" (Surah Al-Hadid 57:21)

You're not racing *against* anyone.

You're racing *toward* Allah.

And He's not waiting to punish you for being slow.

He's waiting to reward you for showing up — even with shaky steps.

A Du'a for This Chapter

Ya Allah…

Protect my heart from comparison.

Let me walk my path with peace and patience.

Let me celebrate others without doubting myself.

Let me grow at my pace — with sincerity, not pressure.

And let me always remember: You see me, You know me, and You are near.

Ameen.

Heart Reflection

Write down one area of your deen where you've struggled to keep up — not because of laziness, but because of life.

Now write a du'a asking Allah to help you love your journey, even if it looks different from those around you.

Begin with:

"Ya Allah, let me honor my own path back to You…"

 Heart Journal #25

What area of your faith do you often compare to others? How can you shift from competition to compassion — for yourself and them?

Chapter 26

How Gratitude Softens the Hard Days

Sometimes it feels easier to complain than to say *Alhamdulillah.*

When your prayers feel unanswered.

When the loneliness creeps in.

When the dunya gets heavy and your heart feels tired.

You wonder:

"How do I be grateful for this?"

This chapter isn't here to guilt you.

It's here to remind you that gratitude isn't about perfection.

It's about shifting your gaze — from what hurts, to the One who heals.

Gratitude Isn't Just for the Good Days

Real gratitude is tested when the blessings aren't obvious.

When you lose a friend — but gain clarity.

When your du'a is delayed — but your patience grows.

When your income tightens — but your trust deepens.

The Prophet  said:

"Amazing is the affair of the believer. For everything there is good — and this is only for the believer. If something good happens, they are grateful, and that is good. If something hard happens, they are patient, and that is good."

(Muslim)

Gratitude isn't pretending everything is perfect.

It's believing that *Allah is still with you*, even when everything feels wrong.

Gratitude Isn't Always Loud — Sometimes It's Just Survival

You may not say *Alhamdulillah* with fireworks and joy.

Sometimes it's whispered with tears.

Sometimes it's just getting out of bed.

Sometimes it's saying, *"I'm still here. And I still believe."*

That, too, is gratitude.

A quiet kind.

But Allah sees it.

The More You Thank Allah, the More You Notice His Gifts

Allah promises in the Qur'an:

"If you are grateful, I will surely increase you…"

(Surah Ibrahim 14:7)

Not just increase you in wealth or ease —
But in *clarity, calm, healing, and light.*

Gratitude softens the hard edges of pain.

It gives you a reason to keep going.

It lifts your eyes from the storm, back to the One who controls the sky.

Start Small: Practice Daily Gratitude as Worship

Try this, even on your hardest days:

- Write down 3 things you're thankful for before bed
- Say *"Alhamdulillah"* after each prayer — and mean it
- Reflect on one du'a that was answered in a way you didn't expect
- Thank Allah for something you take for granted: your breath, your limbs, your tongue that says His name

These small acts change your lens.

And soon, the world begins to feel softer — even if nothing else changes.

✦ Bismillah in the Small Things

One of the simplest, most beautiful ways to bring Allah into your daily life is to say **"Bismillah"** — *In the Name of Allah* — before you do anything.

Before you enter a room. Before you take a bite of fruit. Before you turn on the stove to cook dinner. Before you pick up your phone. Before you start your car. Before you do anything at all.

It's a whisper that reminds your heart: *I'm not doing this alone. I'm doing it with purpose, with blessing, with Allah.*

Even these small acts can become forms of worship when they begin with His Name.

✦ Gratitude in the Everyday

Gratitude isn't just about the big, life-changing moments. It's also in the little mercies that surround you:

🍑 A perfectly sweet fruit.

🍲 A warm meal you didn't have to fight for.

💧 Cool water after a long walk.

🌬 A soft breeze on your face when it's warm.

🌕 The sky stretched wide above you in all its beauty.

Gratitude is whispering *Alhamdulillah* — even when life is hard — because somewhere in the quiet, Allah still gave you something to hold on to.

These moments soften the heart. They remind you: He is near, even in the smallest gifts.

A Du'a for This Chapter

Ya Allah…

Even when I feel broken, let my heart whisper Alhamdulillah.

Even when I ache, let me see Your mercy.

Let me thank You for what I have, and trust You with what I don't.

Fill me with gratitude that protects me from despair.

And let my thanks be a bridge back to peace.

Ameen.

Heart Reflection

What is one trial you've faced recently that shook your heart?

Now write down three blessings — even tiny ones — that existed alongside that hardship.

Write a du'a asking Allah to help you see the mercy that was hidden in your struggle.

Start with:

"Ya Allah, soften my heart with gratitude — even when things are hard…"

❀ Heart Journal #26

List 3 blessings that came alongside a recent hardship. Write a du'a of gratitude that includes both the sweetness *and* the struggle.

____

____

____

____

____

____

____

____

____

____

____

Chapter 27

Finding Strength in Private Acts of Worship

You post nothing.

You don't speak about it.

No one claps. No one even knows.

But still — you raised your hands in the dark and made du'a.

You gave charity that no one saw.

You prayed tahajjud with tired eyes and a trembling heart.

You whispered *Astaghfirullah* after a mistake and meant it.

This chapter is a love letter to those moments —

The ones no one witnesses but Allah.

Because sometimes, the most powerful worship happens in secret.

Not to be seen.

Not to be praised.

But just to be held — by the One who sees everything.

The Prophet  Taught Us the Value of Secrecy

He ﷺ said:

"Seven are shaded by Allah on the Day of Judgment... and among them is a person who gives charity so secretly that his left hand does not know what his right hand has given."

(Bukhari and Muslim)

That's not just about charity.

It's about intention.

It's about sincerity.

It's about worship that's done not for attention — but for intimacy with Allah.

Private Worship Builds Private Strength

When no one is watching, and you still choose Allah — that's when your soul is strengthened.

It's in:

- The quiet du'a on your commute
- The silent istighfar in the middle of your shift
- The secret tears you shed before Fajr
- The little moment you lower your gaze — and no one notices but Allah

These small, private acts aren't small at all.

They're where your heart gets trained.

Where your sincerity is tested.

Where your faith grows roots.

You Don't Need a Platform to Be Powerful

You don't have to be a public speaker, a da'wah influencer, or a community leader to be beloved by Allah.

Your value isn't in how visible your Islam is — it's in how *real* it is.

And sometimes, your worship is at its purest when it's just between you and your Lord.

I remember volunteering in a local community pantry, quietly packing food bags and organizing shelves.

No announcements. No social media. Just work for the sake of helping others.

I also spent time cleaning and organizing the masjid — wiping windows, folding prayer rugs, arranging shoes.

No one clapped. No one posted about it. But *I felt accomplished.*

Because in those moments, I wasn't performing for people — I was serving Allah.

There was peace in the silence.

Dignity in the hidden effort.

And a joy in knowing that what I was doing mattered — even if only to the One who sees everything.

And it's just between you and your Lord.

You Can Start Today — Quietly

Start by:

- Making wudu as an act of peace
- Saying *Bismillah* before meals with mindfulness
- Ending your night with du'a for the ummah
- Giving $1 in secret for Allah's sake

- Praying two rak'ah without telling anyone

It doesn't have to be grand.

You just have to be sincere.

A Du'a for This Chapter

Ya Allah…

Let me love the worship that no one sees.

Let me choose You in the quiet, dark, and stillness.

Let me build strength in secret.

Let my sincerity be my shield.

And let every hidden act bring me closer to You.

Ameen.

Heart Reflection

Think of one act of worship you've done recently that no one else knew about.

How did it feel?

Now write a du'a asking Allah to help you grow your faith through unseen deeds — not for praise, but for closeness.

Start with:

"Ya Allah, help me fall in love with the acts that are only for You…"

 **Heart Journal #27**

Write about a private act of worship you've done that no one else knows about. How did it make you feel? Ask Allah to let you grow even stronger in sincerity.

Chapter 28

Relearning How to Celebrate — Joy in Halal Ways

~

After shahada, many reverts wonder quietly:

What am I allowed to celebrate now?

Am I still allowed to feel joy?

Can I mark birthdays, milestones, and success without guilt?

And when Eid comes around, it can feel unfamiliar.

You scroll through photos of other Muslims celebrating with family, food, and laughter…

And you wonder where you belong in it all.

This chapter is here to remind you:

Islam doesn't take joy away. It gives you a more sacred version of it.

You're Allowed to Feel Joy as a Muslim

Smiling is sunnah.

Gratitude is worship.

Joy is not haram.

The Prophet  said:

"Indeed, Allah is beautiful and loves beauty." (Muslim)

And he ﷺ encouraged joy during Eid, weddings, and community events — in ways that uplifted, not distracted.

Joy isn't only permitted.

It's part of a balanced soul.

What Changes Is the *How*— Not the *Why*

Islam doesn't cancel celebration — it *purifies* it.

You still get to mark special moments.

But now, the focus shifts:

- From extravagance → to gratitude
- From seeking validation → to seeking barakah
- From meaningless parties → to meaningful connection

That means you can:

- Celebrate a Qur'an milestone
- Host a halal potluck
- Mark your shahada anniversary
- Bake a cake for someone you love
- Laugh. Decorate. Dress beautifully — with intention.

This isn't "haram joy."

This is *halal happiness.*

And Allah loves it when you thank Him with your heart and your smile.

You Deserve to Build New Joyful Traditions

Maybe you're the only Muslim in your family.

Maybe your first few Eids were lonely.

You may have to give up old holidays that held good memories.

That grief is valid.

But it doesn't mean you can't create *new joy.*

Start small:

- Make special du'a on your shahada anniversary
- Cook your favorite meal for Eid
- Gift others even if they don't give back
- Keep a "Ramadan box" with items that make you smile
- Invite one or two sisters to a tea night

You can *redefine joy* to reflect who you are now — and where your soul belongs.

A Du'a for This Chapter

Ya Allah…

Help me reclaim joy in ways that honor You.

Let me celebrate the path You chose for me.

Let my smiles carry sincerity.

Let my milestones be drenched in gratitude.

And let my joy be worship in disguise.

Ameen.

Heart Reflection

Think of a joyful moment that felt strange after your shahada — like a holiday, birthday, or family gathering.

Now write a du'a asking Allah to bless your future celebrations in halal, fulfilling, and heartfelt ways.

Start with:

"Ya Allah, let my joy be a reflection of Your mercy…"

❀ Heart Journal #28

What would your ideal Eid, Islamic birthday, or personal celebration look like? How can you invite more joy into your faith without guilt?

Chapter 29

Traveling as a Muslim — New Experiences, New Du'as

There's something powerful about stepping into a new place —

A different city. A distant country. A fresh airport terminal.

But after becoming Muslim, travel changes.

You pack your prayer mat.

You scan for halal restaurants.

You plan your flights around salah.

You walk into unfamiliar lands carrying a very visible identity.

And while it's exciting… it can also feel overwhelming.

This chapter is for the traveler in faith — the one who explores the world while staying rooted in Islam.

Traveling Makes You More Aware of Allah

The Prophet  used to make du'a every time he set out on a journey.

He taught us:

"O Allah, You are the Companion on the journey and the Successor over the family. O Allah, I seek refuge in You from the hardship of travel…"

(Muslim)

Travel opens your eyes — but it also tests your soul.

You feel your need for Allah more deeply:

- When you're in transit and tired
- When you can't find a quiet place to pray
- When you're the only Muslim around

And in that need, your connection becomes more sincere.

Your Iman Might Feel Fragile — But That's Okay

In a new country, surrounded by different customs, it's easy to feel unsure.

You may feel:

- Awkward asking where to pray
- Nervous wearing hijab in unfamiliar places
- Disconnected from your routine

But even the Prophet ﷺ had times of physical movement and spiritual recalibration — like the Hijrah to Madinah.

Faith during travel isn't about perfection.

It's about remembrance.

You remember Allah in the airport lounge.

You remember Him on a mountain.

You remember Him in a hotel room, kneeling in a new direction, trusting He still hears you.

Travel Deepens Your Du'a

There's a special kind of du'a that comes when you're far from home.

You look out the window of a moving car or a plane and your heart whispers things you couldn't say before.

Your heart becomes honest.

Your words become raw.

And you begin to see how every new place carries new blessings — and new tests.

Let travel become your du'a journal.

With every new place, ask:

"What is Allah teaching me here?"

✦ A Moment I'll Never Forget

While traveling with my husband in **Granada, Spain**, we visited the stunning **Alhambra Palace** — a place steeped in Islamic history, even though much of its past has faded into silence.

As we walked through its ancient halls, we searched for a quiet corner. We wanted to pray — just the two of us, no fanfare, no attention. We found a hidden spot, laid down our garments as makeshift prayer rugs, and stood before Allah in the stillness.

We didn't know anyone was watching.

But afterward, a man slowly approached us. He didn't say much — just a gesture, a few quiet words — and we realized he had been observing us. He had been contemplating Islam for some time… and in that moment, something in him shifted.

He asked us how to become Muslim. And right there, under the sky of Andalusia, in the heart of the Alhambra, we gently guided him to say the shahada.

La ilaha illa Allah, Muhammadur Rasul Allah.

It was a moment so unexpected, so humbling, it still gives me goosebumps.

We thought we were just finding a place to pray. But Allah had written something so much greater. Alhamdulillah.

You Carry Islam With You — Gently and Proudly

Whether you're in jeans or jilbab…

Whether you speak Arabic fluently or just know Al-Fatihah…

Whether you blend in or stand out —

You are a traveler who carries faith.

Smile gently. Be kind. Ask for help when you need it.

And know that sometimes, you are the first Muslim someone has ever met.

Even while lost on the street, you might be someone's first da'wah.

A Du'a for This Chapter

Ya Allah…

Let every road bring me closer to You.

Protect me in my journeys.

Let me travel with gratitude, humility, and remembrance.

Let the beauty of this world increase my longing for the next.

And let every stop along the way carry a whisper of Your mercy.

Ameen.

Heart Reflection

Think of a trip you've taken since becoming Muslim — or one you hope to take.

What spiritual memory or du'a came from that journey?

Write a prayer asking Allah to make your travels a source of reflection and spiritual depth.

Start with:

"Ya Allah, guide me wherever I go — and never let me forget You along the way…"

❀ Heart Journal #29

Describe one trip (past or future) and how your Islam shaped that journey. What du'as did you carry with you? What spiritual lesson followed you home?

____

____

____

____

____

____

____

____

____

____

Chapter 30

Facing Big Life Decisions with Tawakkul (Trust in Allah)

You're standing at a crossroads.

A job offer. A marriage proposal. A move to a new city. A hijrah you've been praying for.

And you ask the question that reverts often carry more heavily than others:

"Am I making the right choice — or am I just guessing?"

This chapter is for those moments.

The big decisions. The late-night istikharahs.

The choices that will shape your life.

You Don't Have to Know Everything — You Just Have to Trust

Allah says:

"And whoever relies upon Allah — then He is sufficient for him."

(Surah At-Talaq 65:3)

You don't have to see the full picture.

You don't have to have all the answers.

You just need enough trust to take the next step.

That's tawakkul.

It's not passiveness.

It's not recklessness.

It's *intentional surrender.*

You do your part. You ask. You plan.

Then you hand it all over to the One who knows what you cannot see.

Tawakkul Begins with Istikharah — and Continues with Peace

The du'a of istikharah is one of the most powerful gifts for a believer.

It doesn't guarantee a sign in the sky.

But it *does* center your heart in trust.

When you make istikharah and things start falling into place, move forward.

When they fall apart — don't chase.

That *closed door* is also a mercy.

And that delay you're frustrated by?

It might be your greatest protection.

Even the Prophet ﷺ Faced Uncertainty

The Prophet ﷺ made huge life decisions — with du'a, consultation, and trust.

He migrated. He married. He forgave. He strategized.

And through it all, he relied on Allah more than his own insight.

You're not faithless for feeling scared.

You're just human.

Even the strongest hearts tremble before they leap.

Your Du'as Are Part of the Decision

Before you decide, ask:

- Did I consult Allah?
- Did I seek advice from someone wise and sincere?
- Did I reflect with a clear heart?
- Did I give myself time?

And then say:

"Ya Allah, if it's good — open it. If it's not — take it away and protect me from it."

That's not weakness.

That's power in its purest form.

✦ Turning to Istikhara

One of the most powerful tools Allah gives us when making difficult decisions is the prayer of istikharah.

It's not a magic answer. You may not wake up with a sign. But it's a way of saying with your heart: **"Ya Allah, if this is good for me, make it easy. And if it's not, turn it away — and turn me away from it."**

There's something so freeing about that. About handing the unknown over to the One who knows everything.

I've learned to make istikharah not just for the big, life-altering moments like marriage or travel — but even for job opportunities, friendships, and paths I wasn't sure about.

Sometimes the answer shows up quickly. Other times, things shift slowly, in ways I couldn't have predicted.

But what remains is this quiet confidence: Whatever comes after istikharah is better for me, whether I understand it or not.

It's a prayer of surrender — and a prayer of trust. And it's taught me that the more I consult Allah, the less I panic about the outcome.

A Du'a for This Chapter

Ya Allah…

I don't always know what to choose — but I know I have You.

Guide me when I'm unsure.

Protect me from what isn't good for my dunya or akhirah.

Let me trust You more than I trust myself.

And if I walk into a test, let it lead me back to You.

Ameen.

Heart Reflection

Write about a decision you've been struggling with — past or present.

What are you afraid of? What are you hopeful for?

Then write a du'a asking Allah to hold your hand through every unknown.

Start with:

"Ya Allah, I trust You more than I trust the outcome…"

✿ Heart Journal #30

What decision are you currently praying over? Write down your thoughts, your fears — and then write a du'a releasing the outcome to Allah.

____

____

____

____

____

____

____

____

____

____

____

____

____

____

____

____

____

____

____

____

Chapter 31

Trusting the Timing of Qadr — When Life Doesn't Make Sense Yet

You prayed. You planned. You hoped.

And then… things didn't go the way you wanted. The job didn't work out. The person you wanted to marry disappeared. The visa got denied. You missed Fajr. You messed up again.

And now, you wonder: *"Did I fail? Or was this part of the plan?"*

This chapter is here to remind you: **you can trust the timing of Allah — even when it feels like everything is falling apart.**

Qadr Doesn't Mean You're Powerless — It Means You're Protected

Allah's decree isn't a punishment. It's a map.

Sometimes, the route He takes you on is longer than you expected. Sometimes, you think you're lost — but He's just guiding you through a better path.

The Prophet  said: *"Know that what has passed you by was never going to befall you, and what has befallen you was never going to pass you by."* (Tirmidhi)

That means:

- The closed door was meant to close.
- The delay was part of your training.
- The "no" was protecting you from a bigger "yes" later.

Allah Is Not Random — He Is Precise

Your pain has a purpose. Your delay has wisdom. Your unanswered du'a is still traveling — just in a different direction.

Allah's timing isn't slow. It's *perfect.*

Even the Prophet ﷺ waited 13 years for victory in Makkah. Even Maryam (as) endured public shame before Allah revealed her miracle.

You're not behind. You're *right on schedule* — just not yours. His.

You Can Cry and Still Trust

Trusting Qadr doesn't mean you don't grieve. You can be sad. Confused. Heartbroken.

But deep underneath it all — you whisper: *"Ya Allah, I know You're still in control."*

That's tawakkul. Not the absence of emotion — but the presence of surrender.

✦ A Chapter in My Own Story

After my divorce, I felt like everything had fallen apart. I was remorseful. I blamed myself. I blamed others. I blamed the situation. And somewhere along the way, I quietly decided… *That's it.*

I told myself I wasn't going to marry again. I would just grow old, raise my son, and one day maybe help raise my grandchild. *Who would marry a divorced woman anyway? Who would offer a marriage worth hoping for again?*

But Allah had written something I couldn't see yet.

A new door opened. And behind it was a pious husband — one I couldn't have imagined. Not just him, but a whole new family. Beautiful sisters-in-law. A kind mother-in-law. A life filled with faith, calm, and the kind of love that heals gently.

It made me realize something I now hold close to my heart: **If that painful chapter hadn't happened, I would have never reached this one.** The Qadr I once questioned was the very Qadr that brought me somewhere better.

Now when I look back, I no longer see failure. I see redirection. I see mercy. I see that Allah's plan really was the best — even when it broke my heart at first.

A Du'a for This Chapter

Ya Allah… Help me trust the doors You close. Help me be patient when I don't understand. Let me surrender without bitterness. Let me believe that what's meant for me will find me — not a second too early or too late. And let me trust You, even in the dark. Ameen.

Heart Reflection

Think about something in your life that didn't go the way you hoped.

What might Allah have been protecting you from — or guiding you toward?

Write a du'a asking Allah to help you trust in His plan, even when you don't understand it yet.

Start with: *"Ya Allah, help me surrender to Your wisdom, not just my wishes…"*

❀ Heart Journal #31

Think of a moment in your life when something didn't go your way. Now, reflect: What *might* Allah have protected or redirected you toward? Write a heartfelt prayer of surrender.

____

____

____

____

____

____

____

____

____

____

____

____

____

____

____

____

Chapter 32

Islam in Daily Decisions — From Eating to Earning

When you first enter Islam, it often feels like something separate from your daily life — something you do in between everything else. Salah is scheduled, Qur'an is carved out, du'a is reserved for special moments. Islam lives in the "spiritual" sections of the day.

But slowly, quietly, Islam begins to seep into everything.

You find yourself choosing food with more intention. Speaking more gently. Asking "Is this halal?" not just in food, but in the way you earn your money, spend your time, and speak to people. And one day you realize: *Islam isn't part of your life… it is your life.*

The Beauty of Integrating Islam Into the Mundane

Islam is not just about prayer rugs and masjids. It's in the kitchen, the workplace, your bank account, your tone of voice. Every act — eating, earning, resting, speaking, walking — becomes sacred when it's done with the intention to please Allah.

The Prophet ﷺ said: **"You will not spend anything seeking the pleasure of Allah but that you will be rewarded for it, even the morsel of food you place in your wife's mouth."** — *Sahih al-Bukhari*

Even a bite of food. Even washing the dishes. Even checking on your neighbor. Islam is not something you *have to interrupt your life for.* It *becomes the reason for how you live your life.*

Halal Choices Build Barakah

Choosing halal income, even if it pays less. Choosing honesty at work, even if it's harder. Choosing modesty, even if it's uncomfortable. These choices don't just earn you reward — they bring peace. They build *barakah* in your time, your home, your rizq.

Moment from My Journey

There was a time at work when I was introduced to someone and, instinctively, they extended their hand for a handshake. I gently smiled and said, **"I'm sorry, I don't shake hands with the opposite gender out of respect for my faith."**

My boss, who had never seen this before, looked surprised. Not angry — just surprised. It wasn't a confrontation. It was simply… different.

But that one moment opened up space for dawah. I explained that in Islam, physical boundaries are a form of modesty — not judgment. It's about honoring people and maintaining spiritual principles.

He nodded, and the moment passed. But I walked away proud — not of saying "no," but of saying it kindly, clearly, and without shame.

Let Your Day Be Worship

Islam teaches that *every step* can be ibadah. If you start your day with the intention to live for Allah — then even washing dishes, driving to work, or caring for your family becomes part of your worship.

Say, *"Ya Allah, I'm doing this for You."* And it counts.

A Du'a for This Chapter

Ya Allah... Let me live this life in a way that pleases You. Let my income be halal. Let my efforts be sincere. Let my speech be gentle. And let me remember You not just when I raise my hands... but in every choice I make. Ameen.

Heart Reflection

Think of one part of your life you used to think wasn't connected to Islam — like your job, your meals, your hobbies.

How does seeing it through the lens of faith change how you approach it now?

❀ Heart Journal #32

Write about one "everyday" decision you now make with Islam in mind — even if it seems small. Then write a du'a asking Allah to help you bring more of Him into your daily rhythms.

____

____

____

____

____

____

____

____

____

____

____

____

____

____

____

____

____

____

____

Chapter 33
Finding Role Models in the Seerah

As a revert, you may sometimes feel like no one fully understands your journey. You're navigating cultural differences, learning a new way of life, and often walking a path without a blueprint.

But you're not the first to do this. The Seerah — the life of the Prophet ﷺ and his companions — is filled with stories of people who started from confusion, fear, and change… and found their place in Islam.

You are not walking alone. You are walking in their footsteps.

The Prophet ﷺ Welcomed Reverts With Gentleness

When new Muslims came to the Prophet ﷺ, he didn't demand perfection. He guided them slowly. He answered their questions. He listened.

Bilal (RA) came from slavery. Salman al-Farsi (RA) left his homeland searching for truth. Abu Dharr al-Ghifari (RA) had a fiery personality and a rough start. Khadijah (RA) believed before anyone else — and used her strength to protect Islam. Sumayyah (RA), the first martyr in Islam, held to her faith through torture.

Each one had a story. Each one brought something unique. Each one mattered.

And so do you.

You Don't Have to Be Like Everyone Else

Some reverts feel pressure to conform — to sound, dress, speak, or worship like the people around them.

But the beauty of the Seerah is in its diversity. Some companions were scholars. Some were merchants. Some were poor. Some were wealthy. Some were quiet. Some were warriors. What united them wasn't background — it was *La ilaha illa Allah.*

You don't have to erase who you are. You just have to walk toward Allah — like they did.

You Already Belong

The Prophet ﷺ said: **"The best of you in Jahiliyyah are the best of you in Islam — if they gain understanding."** (*Sahih al-Bukhari*)

Your past doesn't disqualify you. It may be part of what makes you strong in your deen.

You don't need to be born into Islam to be a part of this ummah. You've joined a legacy of seekers, strugglers, survivors, and believers — just like those who stood beside the Prophet ﷺ.

A Du'a for This Chapter

Ya Allah... Let me find strength in the stories of those who came before me. Let me see myself in the companions You honored. Let me walk this path with sincerity — even when I feel different. And let me always know: I belong in this ummah. Ameen.

 Heart Reflection

Which companion's story resonates with you most — and why?

What part of their journey reflects your own?

Heart Journal #33

Write a short letter to a companion whose story inspires you. What would you say to Sumayyah, Khadijah, or Salman al-Farsi if you could?

Then, write a du'a asking Allah to help you embody the qualities you admire in them.

____

____

____

____

____

____

____

____

____

____

____

____

Chapter 34

When You Start to Feel at Peace —
And Don't Know Why

At first, Islam might have felt overwhelming. So many rules. So many expectations. So many changes at once. You may have cried after prayer. Questioned yourself after every mistake. Missed your old life. Felt alone.

But somewhere along the way, something shifted.

You woke up one morning and didn't feel lost. You prayed — and your heart didn't resist. You looked in the mirror wearing hijab, or kufi, or just knowing who you are — and felt a quiet kind of confidence. You walked into the masjid and didn't shrink.

And you realize: *I'm still me… but I feel calmer. Softer. Closer to something whole.*

Peace Doesn't Always Announce Itself

You might expect peace to be loud — like a big emotional breakthrough. But most of the time, it arrives like a whisper.

You stop chasing clarity… and start walking with trust. You stop needing answers… and start accepting the Qadr of Allah. You stop performing faith… and start embodying it.

Peace Is Not Perfection — It's Surrender

You still have doubts. You still forget to pray on time. You still feel disconnected some days. But you're not panicking anymore.

Because you've tasted what it's like to come back — and you know Allah will welcome you each time.

That's peace. That's growth. That's proof your roots are taking hold.

You've Changed — Even If No One Else Sees It

Maybe no one notices the internal shift. Maybe your family still doesn't understand. Maybe your friends still see the old you.

But *you* feel it. That quiet steadiness. That inner space where fear no longer screams. That moment where instead of reacting with anxiety, you pause… and remember Allah.

That's a gift from Him.

A Du'a for This Chapter

Ya Allah… Thank You for the peace I didn't know I was searching for. Thank You for softening what used to feel sharp inside me. Keep me grounded in Your mercy — even when life is loud. And let me walk through this world carrying the calm that comes from knowing You. Ameen.

🍃 Heart Reflection

Think about something that used to feel heavy… but now feels lighter. What changed? Or did *you* change?

Let this chapter be a reminder: the softness you feel now is a sign of your spiritual growth.

 Heart Journal #34

Write about a moment when you felt unexpected calm — even though your situation didn't change.

Was it after prayer? A du'a? A long night of tears?

Capture that moment. Then write a du'a asking Allah to keep that peace growing in your heart.

____

____

____

____

____

____

____

____

____

____

____

____

____

____

____

____

____

Chapter 35

The Power of Intention — Turning the Ordinary Into Worship

One of the most beautiful gifts in Islam is this: **You don't have to do something big to earn reward.** You just need to do it for the right reason.

You can turn cooking into worship. Cleaning into worship. Smiling at someone, walking to work, resting — all of it can become an act of ibadah with a simple intention: *"I'm doing this for the sake of Allah."*

It Starts in the Heart

The Prophet  said: **"Actions are judged by intentions, and every person will get what they intended."** (*Sahih al-Bukhari*)

Your heart whispers to Allah before your body ever moves. That means your intention has weight, even when your actions are small — or imperfect.

Maybe your Qur'an recitation isn't fluent. Maybe you still struggle with consistency in salah. But if your intention is to please Allah, to draw closer to Him, to try... Then you are already on sacred ground.

You Don't Need to Be Seen — You Just Need to Be Sincere

It's easy to feel like you're not doing enough — especially when you see others doing more. But sometimes, a quiet, sincere act carries more reward than a loud, public one.

The moment you silently say *"Ya Allah, this is for You"* — that moment is seen by the One who sees everything.

And that makes it meaningful.

Let Your Whole Life Be Worship

Even washing dishes. Even walking to class. Even changing a diaper, making a meal, or showing up to work tired — if you do it for Allah, it counts.

Say to yourself: *"This is worship." "This is for Him."*

And feel how your burdens become lighter. Because now they have meaning.

A Du'a for This Chapter

Ya Allah… Purify my intentions. Let me live sincerely for You, even when no one else sees me. Let my smallest actions carry the weight of worship. And let my heart whisper to You in every moment of my day. Ameen.

Heart Reflection

Think of one part of your routine that feels "mundane" or unnoticed. How could your niyyah (intention) transform it into something sacred?

 Heart Journal #35

Pick one task you often do — work, errands, family care — and write an intention to turn it into worship. Then reflect: how does doing it "for Allah" change your feeling about it?

Chapter 36

When Your Heart Longs for Jannah

There are days when nothing in this world feels like enough. The food doesn't satisfy. The sleep doesn't refresh. The conversations feel shallow. Even your own efforts in faith feel… small.

And yet, deep in your chest, there's a longing. Not for this world — but for something purer. Something untouched. Something called **Jannah**.

A Place Where the Struggle Ends

Maybe you've lost people you loved. Maybe you carry memories you wish you could rewrite. Maybe you're still trying to forgive — others, and yourself. In Jannah, there will be no grief, no guilt, no flashbacks to what could've been. Only mercy. Only light. Only peace.

Allah says in the Qur'an:

"No soul knows what joy is kept hidden for them as a reward for what they used to do." (Surah As-Sajdah 32:17)

That means even your best imagination — your most beautiful dream — still falls short of what's waiting for you.

Even the Smallest Deeds Are Building It

Every time you choose patience instead of snapping. Every time you pray even when your heart is tired. Every time you give when you feel like you don't have enough.

You're not just checking boxes. You're **planting trees in Jannah**. You're paving a path to gardens, rivers, and homes made of mercy.

And Allah — the Most Generous — is recording it all.

Jannah Belongs to People Like You

You may feel unqualified. You may feel like you're still learning, still stumbling, still starting over.

But Jannah isn't only for scholars or those raised in perfect Islamic homes. It's for anyone who strives sincerely. It's for the one who cried at fajr after missing it. It's for the one who kept making du'a even when it felt unanswered. It's for the one who stayed kind when they were misunderstood.

Jannah is for those who fell — and got back up again.

And yes, dear reader... that means it's for you, too.

Hold On — Paradise Is Worth It

Some days it's hard to hold on to hope. But remember: this life is temporary. It's not the destination — it's the test.

Let your pain be part of your elevation. Let your losses be seeds for gardens you'll one day walk through in barefoot joy. Let your longing be a sign: **your soul remembers where it truly belongs.**

And that place is with Allah. That place is Jannah.

A Du'a for This Chapter

Ya Allah… Let my longing for Jannah guide the way I live. Let every hardship I carry become a reason for mercy. Let me enter Paradise with those I love. Let me rest beneath trees I planted through faith. Let me see You — the One I worshipped through fear, hope, and love. *Let me come home.* Ameen.

 Heart Reflection

Have you ever tasted a moment of peace so sweet, you wished it could last forever?

That was a whisper of Jannah.

Think about what parts of this world you love — and what they might feel like, perfected, in the hereafter.

What would your Jannah look like — not just the scenery, but the feeling? Who do you hope is waiting for you there? What emotions do you never want to feel again?

Heart Journal #36

Write a du'a asking Allah to make Jannah your forever home — and to help you live like someone who's walking toward it.

____

____

____

____

____

____

____

A Gentle Whisper Forward

Closing Reflection

You've made it to the end of this book — but not the end of your journey.

In fact, your journey is just beginning. Every du'a you whisper after this. Every surah you try to memorize. Every sujood you make when no one else is around. Every tear. Every setback. Every quiet victory.

All of it — is part of your roots taking hold.

You may not see how far you've come yet. But Allah does.

There will still be days when your faith feels small. When your tongue hesitates. When the world misunderstands you. When even you misunderstand yourself.

But you now carry something in your chest that wasn't there before. Something that can never be taken away.

La ilaha illAllah.

You belong to the One who made you. And He is not finished with you yet.

Some chapters in this book may have made you cry. Some may have felt too real. Some may have felt too far ahead of you.

But I hope all of them reminded you of this:

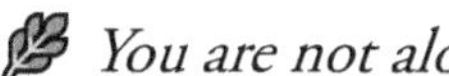

    You are not alone.

    You are not too broken.

🍃 *You are not behind.*

🍃 *You are deeply, deeply loved by the One who guided you.*

Keep going. Keep growing. Keep watering the soil of your soul — with du'a, with dhikr, with patience, with hope.

Let your roots deepen. Let your branches stretch. Let your heart rise — toward the One who never left you, not even for a blink.

And when it gets quiet again… Come back to these pages.

Or better yet — come back to the Qur'an. Come back to the One who called you to Islam in the first place.

He's still here. He always will be.

A Final Du'a for You

Ya Allah… Guide the one reading this book to everything good in this life and the next. Let this journey be filled with ease, even through hardship. Let their faith grow deeper than fear. Let their love for You outweigh all losses. And let their ending be more beautiful than their beginning. Ameen.

With all my love and sisterhood,

Joyful Hijabi